THE WOMBLES GO ROUND THE WORLD

Elisabeth Beresford

Illustrated by Nick Price

GALAXY

PLUS

First published in Great Britain in 2011 by
Bloomsbury Publishing Plc
This Large Print edition published 2012
by AudioGO Ltd
by arrangement with
Bloomsbury Publishing Plc

ISBN: 978 1445 819952

Printed and bound in Great Britain by
MPG Books Group Limited

To Peter, Sarah, Deborah,
William, Thomas and Samantha

PAWS FOR THOUGHT

AN ADDITIONAL NOTE FROM GREAT UNCLE BULGARIA

When I first saw Elisabeth Beresford, I knew that I had met the right Human Being to whom the Womble adventures could be told. It was Boxing Day and she was with her children, Marcus and Kate, walking on Wimbledon Common. They were letting off steam, having had to be on best behaviour over Christmas as their house had been full of elderly relations. I heard Elisabeth's daughter say, 'Oh Ma, it's wonderful on Wombledon Common' and that was it! Elisabeth became aware of our existence, the burrow, and the way we Wombles recycle all the rubbish you Human Beings leave behind.

She told me that she had written lots of children's books, including magic stories, so I told her all about us but I made her promise never to give away the location of the burrow. Since then, we've appeared in books, made records and appeared on television. The young Wombles think it's great fun but I prefer a quiet life. *Tsk, tsk.*

I am very happy to give my pawprint to this reprint (Bungo insisted I use that joke) and hope you enjoy our adventures as much as we did.

Now I must go because Orinoco has just found today's edition of *The Times*. Of course, he has gone straight to the kitchen to claim his reward from Madame Cholet. I think I heard him muttering something about daisy and dandelion fizz . . .

Carry on Wombling.

Great Uncle Bulgaria

CHAPTER 1

ONCE UPON A TIME

'Once upon a time,' said Great Uncle Bulgaria, 'there was a very old, very wise Womble called Great Aunt Thessaly and she lived . . . are you listening, young Bungo?'

'Yes,' said Bungo who, if the truth be told, had been listening with about half of one ear. The other one and a half ears were busy attending to the Womble sitting next to Bungo, because this Womble was making some very strange noises.

'*Erumph, erumph, shhhh*' it sounded like.

'Then what did I just say?' asked Great Uncle Bulgaria, looking very hard at Bungo over the top of his spectacles.

'Once upon a time there was a very old, very wise Womble called Great Aunt Thessaly and she lived,' said Bungo, speaking very fast in a sing-song voice. He nearly added, 'Are you listening, young Bungo?' but for once in his life he acted sensibly

1

and decided not to be cheeky. It was just as well, because Great Uncle Bulgaria had now taken out his second pair of spectacles and put them on the end of his nose, which was a sure sign of trouble for any young Womble who got above him or herself.

'Ho-hum,' said Great Uncle Bulgaria, looking through both pairs of spectacles in a way which made Bungo's fur start to turn prickly.

There was a moment's silence in the Playroom, during which every Womble but one went as still as a field mouse when it senses that an owl is watching it, and then just when Bungo felt he couldn't stand it a second more, the silence was broken by . . .

'ERUMPH, ERUMPH, SHHHH.'

Bang, wallop, crash.

And Orinoco, who had been fast asleep for at least ten minutes, fell off his chair.

'What is it? Who did that? What's happening?' Orinoco asked crossly, rubbing his eyes and patting his nose tenderly where he'd hurt it on the floor. 'Oh sorry, Great Uncle Bulgaria. You'd got to the bit in the story about Great Aunt Thessaly taking you to see Queen Victoria reviewing her soldiers on Wimbledon Common, I expect.'

'No, I had NOT,' replied Great Uncle Bulgaria. He shut the large, important-looking book in front of him and looked at all the young Wombles rather crossly. 'Don't you like me telling you stories any more?' he asked.

'Yes,' said Bungo.

'Mm,' said Tomsk, who is a Womble of few words.

'Rather,' said Orinoco loudly. 'I say, is it time

2

for our late-night acorn juice and bracken buns yet? I'm starving.'

'No, it isn't and no, you are not. *Tiens,* you had three helpings of bramble pie for supper so how, I ask myself, can you be hungry in the least little tiny bit?' demanded Madame Cholet, who had just come into the Playroom for a moment's rest. She had been cooking all day and she was not in the best of tempers.

'Yes, I say, really we do like it,' said Wellington, 'we like Womble stories very much, Great Uncle Bulgaria. The only trouble is that . . . sorry.'

'Sorry about *what*?' asked Great Uncle Bulgaria.

Wellington took a deep breath which misted up his spectacles, so that he had to take them off and wipe them clean on the end of Orinoco's scarf, before he could go on, in a rather muffled voice.

'Well,' said Wellington very bravely, 'we know all the Womble stories off by heart because we've heard them so often. And . . .' Wellington took an even deeper breath, during which Orinoco kindly removed his friend's spectacles, cleaned them and returned them and Great Uncle Bulgaria waited impatiently, 'the stories are all about long ago and—er—rather *old* Wombles, you see. There's nothing about us. Sorry.'

'Dear me,' said Great Uncle Bulgaria, 'dear, dear me. Well, well. I see. Ho-hum.'

'Is it time for our late-night bracken buns and acorn juice yet?' asked Tobermory, putting his head round the door.

Madame Cholet looked from one Womble face to another and got to her back paws.

'Yes, I believe so,' she said. 'Come everybody, and Orinoco, please don't push to the front of the

3

queue, hm?'

'What's the matter, Bulgaria old friend?' asked Tobermory, when everybody else had left the Playroom. 'I thought you always enjoyed reading stories to the young Wombles of an evening, but tonight you look properly down in the dumps.'

'I feel old, Tobermory, old.'

'Well, you *are* old, very old,' said Tobermory reasonably. 'I mean nobody could call getting on for three hundred exactly *young*, now could they?'

'Old and out of date, just like this book,' said Great Uncle Bulgaria, giving *The Womble History of the World, Vol. Nine*, a thump with his white paw.

'Steady on,' said Tobermory and he took the enormous book away and dusted it down carefully with a duster which he kept in his apron pocket. 'Lovely bit of binding that, but it's getting a bit dry and cracked which isn't to be wondered at, seeing as how it's about a hundred years old, if not more. I'll get young Shansi to give it a rub up with a touch of buttercup oil. Very neat with her paws is Shansi. Sorry, you were saying?'

'I was saying I felt old and out of date. In fact, useless,' said Great Uncle Bulgaria, who was working himself up into quite a state as he rocked backwards and forwards in his chair, which began to creak alarmingly.

'That'll need repairing next if you carry on like this,' said Tobermory.

'It's a pity you cannot repair *me*,' said Great Uncle Bulgaria, 'but alas I'm . . .'

'I know, I know, out of date, useless, et cetera, et cetera.' Tobermory stopped rubbing *Vol. Nine* and looked searchingly at his old friend. He had been mending the latch on the outside of the

4

Playroom door and so he had heard everything that had happened; and now, putting two and two together and—being Tobermory—adding it up correctly, he saw exactly what the trouble was. The young Wombles were bored with hearing the same old stories over and over again; they wanted to hear new and exciting tales about the present-day Wombles. They wanted adventures and thrills, but how was he going to get Great Uncle Bulgaria to see this? Rather as Wellington had done, Tobermory took a deep breath and decided to jump in at the deep end. He did it very cunningly.

'Oh well,' said Tobermory in an offhand sort of voice, 'if you really feel as old and worn out as all that, Bulgaria, there's only one thing for it. You'll have to retire. Now let me see, who could we get to come and run the burrow for us?'

'Retire! Run the . . .'

'Now there's Botany, for one. He's getting a bit white in the fur of course and he's all wrapped up in his gardening experiments, but I must say he keeps those little greenhouses of his a treat. Always neat and tidy. No problems for me there, I'm glad to say.'

'Botany!' exclaimed Great Uncle Bulgaria, sitting bolt upright. 'Why, he'd have the burrow full of potted this and seed trays of that before you could say "Womble". He's already installed the underwater farming tanks as it is!'

Tobermory pulled a clipboard out of his apron pocket, took a pencil from behind his ear and began to write busily as he went on.

'All right, I must admit I have to agree with you there. Botany might very well turn the burrow into a sort of underground greenhouse. So we'll cross

5

him off. Ah, but have you considered Cousin Yellowstone as your successor? Now there, you must agree, is a very efficient Womble. Runs his burrow in the States by computer, so I believe. Clockwork computer, that is. Yellowstone's Wimbledon Common bred don't forget and I dare say he'd like to come home again. And what's more,' said Tobermory, carefully avoiding Great Uncle Bulgaria's eyes which were now looking not at all old, but very bright and frosty indeed, 'what's more, I have heard that Yellowstone's thinking of writing some new, modern Womble stories. What do you say to Yellowstone taking over?'

'Never,' said Great Uncle Bulgaria, thumping his stick on the ground. 'Clockwork computers indeed! Why, they waste more time than they save. And what do you mean, new, *modern* Womble stories?'

'Oh, just bringing Womble History up to date,' said Tobermory vaguely. 'You know how American Wombles like that kind of thing. All right, so I'll cross out Yellowstone. Which leaves . . .'

'Leaves who?' said Great Uncle Bulgaria in a very ominous tone of voice.

'The MacWomble, who else? Cairngorm, the MacWomble the Terrible of the Loch Ness Burrow. He's got plenty of energy and enthusiasm and he's young yet. Not more than two hundred, if he's a day. Yes, Bulgaria, he might just be the Womble for the job. And being Scotch—sorry, Scottish—he'd be keen to write a new History. They like that kind of thing up in Scotland too, I believe,' said Tobermory even more vaguely, as he hadn't the least idea if they did or not.

'Never, NEVER, NEVER!' said Great Uncle

6

Bulgaria, quite forgetting that he was old and out of date and useless. In fact he roared the last 'never' so loudly that Shansi, who was just bringing in a tray loaded with bracken buns and acorn juice, dropped it in the doorway.

'Stupid little Womble,' snapped Great Uncle Bulgaria rather unfairly, 'pick that up. Return to the kitchen and tell everybody that I have an Important Announcement to make.'

'Yes, Great Uncle Bulgaria,' whispered Shansi, and she did as she was told and scuttled off as fast as her back paws would carry her.

'What announcement, then?' asked Tobermory, wiping his grey moustache with the duster in order to hide the fact that he was trying not to smile.

'Wait and see,' snapped Great Uncle Bulgaria, jumping out of his chair and beginning to march up and down the Playroom. 'Really you can be almost stupid at times, old friend. It's all as plain as a tidy-bag. We have been living in the past. Who wants to hear the same old stories over and over

7

again when there is so much happening in the present? There are so many new chapters to be added to *The Womble History of the World*. There is, for example, the adventure of Bungo and the spotted dog . . .' [See *The Wombles.*]

'Tomsk and the Snow Womble . . .'

'The occasion when Orinoco ran away to Fortune and Bason . . .'

'The arrival of Cousin Yellowstone . . .'

'The time when we had to leave the Wimbledon Common Burrow and I was in charge of getting all of us to Hyde Park . . .' [See *The Wandering Wombles.*]

'After Bungo and Orinoco had gone up to Scotland and been captured, so to speak, by the Scotch, sorry, Scottish Wombles . . .'

'When Tomsk was nearly arrested outside Buckingham Palace and Wellington saved him . . .'

'Let alone all the troubles we had when we got to Hyde Park and that Russian Womble came under the wire from Kensington Gardens. Now what was his name?' said Tobermory, scratching behind his ear with his pencil [See *The Wombles at Work.*]

'Omsk. And don't forget, Tobermory, what difficulties we faced when we finally returned to our Wimbledon Common Burrow. You remember how it ended up—with far more of us returning than I had first expected. Why, even I myself became homesick for Wimbledon!'

'*Tsk, tsk, tsk,*' said Tobermory, 'it really is remarkable what a lot has happened to us Wombles, one way and another. Why, I don't believe I can remember the half of it.'

'No, I don't suppose you can,' agreed Great

Uncle Bulgaria, 'but fortunately I have always kept up my diary, in which I write down everything. Which reminds me, Tobermory, I made a note only this morning that my rocking chair needs oiling. You might see to it as soon as you can, my good Womble. I don't want the thing squeaking and squawking while I'm trying to concentrate.'

'Yes, Bulgaria,' said Tobermory, who was so relieved to see his old friend being busy and important again, that he nobly didn't mention that he'd been the one who had referred to the poor state of the rocker only a couple of minutes ago.

'Good, good. I know I can always rely on *you*, Tobermory. You are always needed here at Wimbledon, just as I am. Although perhaps not *quite* as much. Which makes it all very difficult. Whom shall I send?'

'Send?' asked Tobermory cautiously. 'Send where? I say, we're not going to have to move again, are we? I never did like that Hyde Park burrow. Too draughty by half.'

'No, no, no, no. I wonder if I might borrow that writing board of yours and that pencil? Thank you so much. Well, come along, Tobermory, don't just stand there with your mouth open. There's not a moment to lose.'

With these words Great Uncle Bulgaria seized the clipboard and the pencil and with *The Womble History* under his other arm, he marched out of the Playroom. Tobermory shut his mouth with a snap which made his bowler hat fall over his eyes and followed, muttering under his breath, 'Oh lor, oh dear, now what's he up to? I was only trying to get him out of the doldrums. I didn't mean him to get all fired up. The next thing you know he'll have us

9

all going to the moon, or some such nonsense, and asking me to make a clockwork rocket . . .oh dear, oh dear . . .'

In the kitchen everybody was stuffing the last of their bracken buns into their mouths and whispering. Nobody, not even Orinoco or the smallest Womble from the Womblegarten, looked in the least sleepy or bored, as they all had that prickly feeling in their fur which meant that something interesting and exciting was about to happen.

'I do like Important Announcements,' said Alderney to her great friend Shansi.

'I don't,' said Shansi, 'not very much really. They make me drop trays.'

'Well, nothing was broken, little one,' said Madame Cholet, 'so please stop worrying. Ah-HA, Monsieur Bulgaria arrives. Now we shall see what we shall see. *N'est-ce pas?*'

Having a French name, Madame Cholet likes to speak French from time to time.

'Wombles,' announced Great Uncle Bulgaria, 'I have made an important, a *very* important decision. It was pointed out to me tonight by some of you young Wombles that *The Womble History of the World, Vol. Nine*, was old-fashioned and out of date.'

Wellington gulped and half swallowed a crumb, but luckily, before he could choke, he was hit on the back by Tomsk.

'And those young Wombles were quite right,' went on Great Uncle Bulgaria. 'I only wish that they had mentioned it to me before. One is never too old to learn, whatever some of you may think. Therefore I have decided that we Wombles of

10

Wimbledon shall bring things up to date. *We* are going to write *Vol.* TEN.'

Everybody looked at everybody else and then back again.

'What a smashing idea. Sorry, good idea. I like writing things,' said Wellington.

'I don't,' said Bungo.

'It's very hard sort of work,' muttered Orinoco.

'Mm,' agreed Tomsk.

'Good writing is most important,' said Miss Adelaide, who is in charge of the Womblegarten.

'Writing out recipes is all right,' said Alderney.

'I could do the pictures, perhaps?' suggested Shansi.

'Thank you,' said Great Uncle Bulgaria, 'of course, I shall do most, if not all, of the writing concerning what has happened to us Wimbledon Wombles. We have had so many adventures one way and another, but they will only be a part of *Vol. Ten.* You see, if a great many exciting things have occurred *here*, it must follow that Wombles all over the world will also have thrilling stories to tell. Don't you agree?'

There was a buzz of agreement after everybody had thought this over.

'Therefore,' said Great Uncle Bulgaria, when all the nodding and muttering and whispering had died down, 'I think, I believe, I *know* that it is up to some of us Wimbledon Wombles to collect all those exciting stories—from burrows everywhere.'

'Oh dear, oh lor,' muttered Tobermory. '*Now* what?'

Madame Cholet passed him three bracken buns and a mug of hot acorn juice and went, '*Shhh.*'

'So,' went on Great Uncle Bulgaria, 'this is my

11

Important Announcement. I want four Womble volunteers to travel round the world and find out what has been happening to all the other Wombles. It will be interesting, it will be exciting and it may even be dangerous. Well?'

There was a moment's silence and then Bungo and Tomsk put up their paws, followed closely by Wellington. Orinoco, who had dozed off for a second, wondered sleepily if anybody was being asked if they would like another bun and put up his paw.

'Bungo, Tomsk, Wellington, Orinoco,' said Great Uncle Bulgaria. 'Congratulations. You are about to start on the Greatest Womble Adventure of your lives. Report to my study at nine o'clock sharp tomorrow morning. Tobermory, I'd like a word with you.'

CHAPTER 2

BACK TO SCHOOL

'I wish you'd told me what was happening,' grumbled Orinoco. 'I thought Great Uncle Bulgaria was asking if anybody wanted another bun. I didn't know he was talking about going to foreign countries and *if* I'd known, I jolly well wouldn't have said yes.'

'Well, you didn't, he was and you have,' replied Bungo, who was bursting with excitement and energy. He took a quick look round the Common to see if there were any Human Beings about but, as it was six o'clock on a cold, wet, grey morning, there wasn't a sign of one. In fact, the only movement to be seen was a small, round figure jogging across the skyline.

'Tomsk doing his morning run,' said Bungo, and he put down his tidy-bag and did a backward somersault out of sheer high spirits.

'I wish you wouldn't do that,' said Orinoco, who

13

was in a really bad mood. 'It makes me tired just watching you.'

'Shut your eyes then,' said Bungo and did another one; but, because he wasn't looking where he was going, he flipped straight into a bramble bush.

'Ouch, help,' shouted Bungo, making a clutch for his cap which had been jerked off his head.

'You do look funny,' said Orinoco, starting to laugh.

'Lend us a paw, there's a good Womble,' said Bungo, jumping up and down as he tried to grab his cap which was bobbing about just out of reach.

'He-he-he, ho-ho-ho, ha-ha-ha,' wheezed Orinoco, clutching his stomach. 'Go for it, Bungo.'

'And what do you think you're playing at?' asked a quiet voice, which made Orinoco stop laughing and Bungo stop bouncing in half a second flat.

'If you've quite finished wasting time, then kindly return to the burrow at once; Tobermory is waiting for you,' went on Great Uncle Bulgaria and he reached up with his stick, tweaked the cap free and dropped it on to Bungo's head. Then he held out the handle to Bungo and pulled that young Womble out of the bush with no trouble at all.

'Burrow!' said Great Uncle Bulgaria and pointed in that direction. Off went the two young Wombles at a fast jog-trot.

'Isn't it strange,' gasped Bungo, 'that Great Uncle Bulgaria always seems to be in places where you don't expect him!'

'Mm,' replied Orinoco who, because he's rather fat, can't talk and run at the same time.

'Ho, ho, ho,' said Great Uncle Bulgaria, having

14

a quiet little laugh on his own. 'I must admit Bungo did look very funny. Stupid sort of name, Bungo, but it does suit him!'

In the Workshop, Tobermory was surrounded by full tidy-bags which he was sorting out in his usual efficient way. Standing beside him was Shansi with a notebook and a pencil.

'Newspapers, three. Good, there's a copy of yesterday's *Times*. Put that on one side for Great Uncle Bulgaria. Milk bottles, four: kitchen for Madame Cholet. Yoghurt cartons, six: Cousin Botany for seed pots. Pieces of paper and paper bags, various: Miss Adelaide for the Womblegarten. Tin cans . . .' Tobermory stopped speaking and looked up as Bungo and Orinoco came in and put down their tidy-bags.

'So there you are,' he said. 'Now, I want you two to go straight to the Womblegarten, where you'll report to Miss Adelaide.'

'The Womblegarten!' said Orinoco. 'But that's for *little* Wombles. Not for working Wombles like us who do tidying-up.'

'Ah, but things are changing,' said Tobermory, his little round eyes twinkling. 'You see, according to Great Uncle Bulgaria's latest orders, you working Wombles are going back to school, while the little Wombles are to learn tidying-up.'

Orinoco and Bungo, who for once in their lives were quite unable to speak at this extraordinary news, looked at each other and then back at Tobermory.

'Orders are orders,' he said. 'Off with you, and don't keep Miss Adelaide waiting. Now, then, Shansi, what have we here? One saucepan, bad condition: Workshop. Three gloves, various . . .'

15

'The Womblegarten,' grumbled Orinoco. 'Fancy having to go back to school! I don't like this new adventure at all. It sounds too much like hard work to me. I wish I'd never . . .'

'Put your paw up, I know. But it may not be too bad,' said Bungo.

Wellington and Tomsk were already sitting at desks with notebooks made of ironed-out paper bags in front of them. Miss Adelaide was standing at the side of a large map of the world with a stick in her paw. She looked over her spectacles at the latecomers and nodded to them to sit down.

'Attention please, Wombles,' she said. 'As from this moment you are released from tidying-up duties . . .' Orinoco's face brightened and then fell as Miss Adelaide went on, 'so that you can concentrate on learning about the countries to which you will travel. Great Uncle Bulgaria and I have made out your itineraries.'

'Itin—?' said Tomsk, who wasn't at all sure what was happening.

'Travel plans. You, Tomsk, will travel with Wellington. You did quite well when you worked together before.'

'Oh yes, when we went to Buckingham Palace and I was a Guardwomble,' said Tomsk. 'I remember. I wore a uniform and Wellington . . .'

'Exactly. Precisely, but we won't go into that now. And you, Orinoco, will travel with Bungo, because Bungo has plenty of energy while you Orinoco are—sometimes—quite sensible. Wellington, as we all know, is *extremely* sensible.'

'Oh, I say, sorry, but . . .' muttered Wellington.

'But inclined to be absent-minded,' went on Miss Adelaide. Wellington sighed and nodded.

16

Sometimes he even got lost on Wimbledon Common, so how was he going to manage to find his way in the big wide world?

'I'll keep an eye on him,' rumbled Tomsk, who rarely worries about anything as he's always pretty certain that difficulties, no matter how scaring, will be overcome in the end.

'ATTENTION please,' said Miss Adelaide, tapping the map with her stick. 'Now as you can see, I have divided the world into two parts—with this black line down the middle—so that you will have half each. Understood?'

The four young Wombles nodded speechlessly. It sounded so grand to be given 'half the world' to cover.

'Bungo and Orinoco, you will go west to America . . .'

'Oh good, that means seeing Cousin Yellowstone again,' said Bungo, who had always got on very well with his American cousin.

'Good sort of Womble,' agreed Orinoco. 'I remember when I kind of met him outside the back door of Fortune and Bason and . . .'

'We *all* remember it,' said Miss Adelaide. 'We can also recall *why* you happened to be there in the first place. Shall I proceed, or would you prefer to take over this lesson?'

There was absolute stillness and silence in the Womblegarten.

'Thank you *so* much,' said Miss Adelaide with the quiet politeness which had been known to make even Great Uncle Bulgaria stop talking. 'After you have finished working with our American cousins, you will travel even further west to Japan. If, Wellington, you were about to point

17

out that Japan is normally considered to be to the east, I would remind you that Japan is to the *west* of America. When your work is finished there you will proceed home to Wimbledon. Any questions?'

'Please, yes, sorry, but *how* are we travelling?' asked Wellington anxiously.

'We're not walking, are we?' Orinoco said in a horrified voice. 'I mean America's even further away than Scotland . . . I think.'

'I sometimes wonder,' said Miss Adelaide, 'if you ever paid any attention at all during your time in the Womblegarten. Unless you had webbed paws like our Water-Womble cousin, Nessie of Loch Ness, you would find it extremely difficult to *walk* to America. Please look at the map.'

'Oh yes,' said Orinoco after a pause, 'there's all that sea to cross.'

'The Irish Channel and the Atlantic Ocean to be precise. No, I do not, as yet, know how you will travel. That is Tobermory's department, not mine. He is now, I understand, T.O.W.' And Miss Adelaide gave a slight cough behind one silky grey paw.

'I didn't think you spelt Tobermory like that,' said Tomsk, who was getting more puzzled by the minute.

'You don't. T.O.W. stands for Transport Officer Womble. You, Tomsk, together with Wellington will travel eastwards, calling in on various Womble burrows in Europe before proceeding still further to Australia and New Zealand. Any questions?'

The four young Wombles stared silently at Miss Adelaide. All their four sets of eyes had a glazed look and all four mouths were open, and for one pin, let alone two, they would have liked very much

18

to stop being volunteers and to go straight back to nice, ordinary tidying-up work.

'*Tsk, tsk, tsk,*' said Miss Adelaide bracingly, 'you are now old enough to go out in the world and to have proper exciting adventures. Why, Cousin Yellowstone was only young when he ran away to sea—on his own—and worked his way right round the globe. And look at Cousin Botany: he went to sea too, [See *The Womles to the Rescue*] although I must admit that he did it by mistake—and that was in a sailing ship as a stowaway. Then there was the Great MacWomble Chieftain who helped Bonnie Prince Charlie and Flora Macdonald to escape from the soldiers. And there are many, many more Wombles who have performed all kinds of brave acts. Don't you want to be like them, or would you prefer to stay here just being snug and comfortable?'

'Yes,' said Wellington honestly, 'I would, because I'm not a brave sort of Womble myself. But well . . . all right, perhaps it won't be too bad having adventures . . . I hope.'

'Of course, it won't. It will be most interesting and, what is more, those adventures will all be written down and put into *Vol. Ten*. You may very well become famous, in a minor kind of way.'

'I'd *like* to be famous,' said Bungo. 'I'd like Wombles everywhere to read about *me*.'

'I thought you might. Ah, listen, I think I can hear the trolley coming. You may have a ten-minute break. No more than three sandwiches, Orinoco; we want you to be fit not fat.'

Alderney came bouncing into the classroom, pushing the trolley with her cap over one eye and her apron fluttering.

'Morning, Miss Adelaide. Madame Cholet said, please could you please spare her a minute in the kitchen. I say,' she straightened her cap and looked at Orinoco, Bungo, Wellington and Tomsk, 'it's not fair. You *are* lucky. I wish it was me that was going off travelling and meeting all our Womble relations. I say, wouldn't one of you swap with me? It's really not bad working in the kitchen and doing the washing-up, you know. And I would love to go and have adventures and see new countries and all that. Well?'

Now such is Womble nature that the moment Alderney uttered these words the four reluctant volunteers immediately changed their minds about the whole business.

'Sorry, awfully sorry, but no,' said Wellington.

Tomsk shook his head.

'Rather *not*,' said Bungo.

'Can't be done,' said Orinoco. 'You see, I've just had a jolly good idea. I'm going to collect Womble recipes round the world. I'm sure Madame Cholet would be very interested. Of course, I'm only going to do it for her.'

'Oh bother,' said Alderney. 'Oh well, never mind then. But next time, when we get to *Vol. Eleven*, I'm going to volunteer before anybody else. Who wants a buttercup relish sandwich?'

Miss Adelaide, who had been hovering in the doorway, smiled gently and made her way to the kitchen, where Madame Cholet handed her a steaming mug of acorn juice.

'And how does it go?' enquired Madame Cholet.

'It goes *comme ci comme ça*, but there is a great deal of work to be done before our young Wombles are ready to face what lies ahead. Are those daisy cream buns I see? Well, perhaps just one—or maybe two. *Merci*, Madame Cholet.'

Miss Adelaide, who like Great Uncle Bulgaria has an uncanny gift for nearly always being right about everything, was right again. There *was* a great deal to be done and during the next few weeks the four volunteers hardly knew whether they were on their front or their back paws. There was Geography and History to be learnt about the countries which they were to visit.

'What is the capital city of Australia, Tomsk?'

'Melbourne, no, er—Sydney? No—er Canberra?'

'Correct. Canberra. Name the oldest Australian Womble burrow, Wellington.'

'Er, sorry, oh yes, the Great Outback Burrow. Great-great Aunt M. Murrumbidgee is in charge.'

'Correct. Bungo, this is for you. Who is Cousin Yellowstone's assistant?'

'Um. Idaho.'

'Quite right. Tomsk, the collective name of the first Wombles you will meet in France?'

Tomsk rolled his eyes, made a dreadful face and then rumbled, 'Les WombleauX, BouloGNE.'

'Yes. But they do not pronounce the "X", neither do they say *"BOLOGNEE"*. Say after me: *"les Wombleaux* of Boulogne". And again, please. Good. Orinoco, tell me the name of the most important Womble in Japan and the date when the burrow was started.'

'Honourable Cousin Tokyo and—oh—er—um—about . . .' Orinoco looked round desperately for help.

'*Tsk, tsk, tsk*. You must attend, Orinoco. I shall take you through Womble Japanese history once

21

more. It was in . . .'

While all this was going on, Tobermory was crashing and banging away in his experimental Workshop, which now had a little notice pinned on the door that said:

T.O.W.
PLEASE KEEP OUT
UNLESS URGENT

'How is it going, old friend?' asked Great Uncle Bulgaria, putting his head round the door.

'Not too badly,' replied Tobermory. 'That is, not too well either.' Tobermory always prefers to look on the black side of things.

'Of course, of course. Transporting two lots of young Wombles round the world, and in opposite directions, must be a very difficult problem.'

'Yes, it is. And it's not as if I hadn't got enough to do already. Don't forget, Bulgaria, I have to keep the burrow going and deal with all the rubbish that's tidied up as well as being T. O. whatsit. I don't know how to manage it all and that's a fact. Have a seat.'

Great Uncle Bulgaria nodded politely and sat down on a packing case which had ... YFFES BANANAS printed on it. He leant forward on his stick and looked at Tobermory over the top of his spectacles.

'Is it really all too much for you?' he asked gently.

' 'Course it's not,' replied Tobermory, pushing back his bowler hat with a screwdriver. 'I like trying to solve problems. Ah-HEM, that is, when there's not too many of 'em. I must say though that little Shansi has been a great help. She's got an orderly kind of mind, that young Womble. Doesn't get flustered, no matter how much work we've got on hand. *Tsk, tsk, tsk.*'

'Good. Well?'

'Ah,' said Tobermory, scratching harder than ever, 'it's how to get them round the world that's the difficulty. Well, I thought of a boat, of course, because they'll be travelling over the sea a lot, but then I said to myself, well once they've *been* over the sea and come to land, what next? They'll be met, no doubt, by our Womble relations, so then what?'

'More travelling?' suggested Great Uncle Bulgaria.

'That's it. That's it exactly. You see, Bulgaria, that's what all this is about. Hearing stories, collecting information, I suppose you could call it, and then moving on again. And they won't just be going across water, they'll be crossing land as well. So I thought to myself . . . I hope I'm not boring you?'

'Never. I'm fascinated. Please proceed.'

'Ah. So I said to myself, what about a boat that turns into a kind of car. But,' said Tobermory and stopped dead.

'But?'

'Well, I said to myself, travelling by car-boat might take a lot of time and trouble. So,' Tobermory took a deep breath, 'I thought of something quite different—like going by air.'

'You mean by aeroplane?'

'No, I don't. Noisy, wasteful things, aeroplanes.

23

For a start they use up all that fuel and then they leave dirty marks all over the sky. I wouldn't soil my paws with them—that is, not until I've thought of a different sort of aeroplane. *If* I ever have the time.'

'You're not contemplating a *rocket*, Tobermory?'

'No, no, no, that'd be even worse. What flies through the air without making a sound, Bulgaria?'

'An owl?' suggested Great Uncle Bulgaria. 'Very silent birds in flight, owls. But I don't quite see how . . .'

'Owls!' said Tobermory in a contemptuous tone of voice. 'Silly sort of birds they are, in spite of them being supposed to be so wise. I never met an owl yet you could exchange a sensible word with. *Too-whit* and *too-whoo* is all they ever have to say for themselves. No, no, no, Bulgaria, you've got it quite wrong. Look here, I'll show you.'

And Tobermory pulled out a large piece of cardboard which was covered in drawings and plonked it down on the Workshop bench. Great Uncle Bulgaria got up and went to look at it. He looked at it for quite a long time in silence and then he said, 'A balloon!'

'A clockwork balloon.'

'Tobermory,' said Great Uncle Bulgaria, 'you— you are a genius!'

'No, just practical. But there is one slight problem,' said Tobermory, scratching his head again, 'and that is, Bulgaria, will it work? Will the thing actually fly? Between you and me and the front door, I'm not too certain that it will, which is why I'm having a test flight early tomorrow morning, before anyone is about. But I hope *you'll* come and watch?'

CHAPTER 3

HE FLIES THROUGH THE AIR

In some mysterious way word soon got round the burrow with the result that, when Tobermory emerged on the Common pushing a very large basket-ware trolley and wearing a zip-up jacket and a crash helmet (over his bowler), there were Wombles everywhere. But they were, so to speak, invisible. This was because Great Uncle Bulgaria had set his alarm clock for 5.30 a.m. exactly. By 5.38 he had realised what was happening and had given everyone a short sharp whispered lecture, in which he said that Tobermory might feel a bit shy about trying out his latest invention, if he knew that he had a large audience.

'Tobermory—shy?' said Orinoco, blinking and yawning.

'Shy!' said Great Uncle Bulgaria. 'So, if you want to watch what is going to happen, please do so from hidden positions. Off with you.'

They went.

It was cold and grey and damp out on the Common, but nobody made a sound as Tobermory bumped his trolley across the grass to where Great Uncle Bulgaria, wearing two shawls, was waiting for him.

'Lovely morning,' said Tobermory.

'Yes, indeed.'

'Well, here we are then. It's a funny thing you know, Bulgaria, but I've never actually flown before. I dare say it'll be an interesting experience. Hold that for me would you?'

'Certainly.'

Tobermory produced various bits of this and that out of the trolley and whistled softly under his breath, making little puffs of steam in the cold air.

'I'd never let any other Womble try out a machine that I hadn't thoroughly tested myself,' Tobermory went on, breathing rather faster as he began to use a foot pump. Something which up until now had looked like a flat, grey carpet began to heave and swell.

'Quite right too,' agreed Great Uncle Bulgaria.

'There she goes,' said Tobermory as the grey shape was transformed into a large, almost round balloon. 'Hold on tight, Bulgaria. She'll start tugging in a moment.'

'I rather think she is already, Tobermory.'

'Hang on carefully then,' commanded Tobermory, suddenly forgetting to be rather anxious as he saw his latest invention surging into life. He hurried round adjusting things and going 'tsk, tsk, tsk,' under his breath, and then he climbed into the trolley and bent down. There was a click-click-click sound. Great Uncle Bulgaria held his

26

breath and so did all the other Wombles. An aeroplane roared overhead on its way to Heathrow Airport, but nobody took the slightest bit of notice as they were far too interested in what was happening on Wimbledon Common. The circular balloon was now hovering and tugging some ten feet above the trolley. It really looked as if it were longing to get up into the sky.

'Now!' commanded Tobermory, suddenly bobbing up. 'Let her out slowly, Bulgaria.'

Great Uncle Bulgaria did his best, but one moment he was carefully paying the rope out and the next the rope was behaving as though it had come to life and was fairly whizzing through his paws.

'Wombles—assistance!' roared Great Uncle Bulgaria. Fortunately for him, Tomsk happened to be the one who was the closest and he catapulted out of the bush where he'd been hiding, pounded across the grass and caught up with Great Uncle Bulgaria—who was trotting along at a remarkable speed for a Womble of his age—in a vain effort to hold on to the fast-vanishing end of the rope.

Tomsk did his best-ever rugger tackle and just caught the rope end at the exact moment that it snaked out of Great Uncle Bulgaria's front paws. There was a tremendous jerk on Tomsk's arms but he hung on tightly, his feet going so fast that they were just a blur of motion. Then the pull on his arms grew even more powerful and to his great alarm Tomsk realised that, although he was still running extremely fast, his feet were no longer touching anything.

'Heelp!' roared Tomsk breathlessly and looked down. He gasped, gulped, shut his eyes tightly and hung on for all he was worth. There was nothing much else he could do, for the Common was already at least twenty feet below him.

'Funny,' said Tobermory, who had sat down with a bump in the bottom of the trolley because of the jerky take-off. 'She isn't going up as fast as I thought she would with only one aboard. I must have made a mistake somewhere. Better make a few adjustments.'

The speed of the two clockwork propellers increased, going *clickety-click*-CLACK, *clickety-click*-CLACK.

'Must make a note of that,' muttered Tobermory, getting his clipboard out of his apron pocket and writing busily. 'Hallo, *now* what? If it isn't one thing, it's another. She's swaying a bit . . .'

Tobermory looked over the edge of the trolley and watched the Common swinging backwards and forwards. Dotted all over the grass were dozens of small, round, furry figures, dancing about on their back paws and waving and pointing.

'I thought I'd made it clear to Bulgaria that I didn't want an audience,' grumbled Tobermory. 'Oh well,' and being polite, as all Wombles are, he waved back.

The figures down below waved back even more frantically.

'Lot of nonsense,' said Tobermory. 'It's nothing to get so worked up about. After all, this is only the first clockwork balloon flight in the world. Nothing special really. I'd better take a few more readings and . . . hallo, what's that then?'

'Heeeeelp,' cried a despairing voice from below.

Tobermory leant dangerously far over the edge of the trolley and looked down at the Common, which was dipping backwards and forwards in a manner which made Tobermory begin to feel distinctly air-sick.

'Shtabilishers,' he said with one paw over his mouth. 'Should have thought of that for rough weather. Only it's quite calm this morning and OH MY WORD!'

Tobermory forgot his queasy stomach—in fact, he forgot almost everything, as into his line of vision came the end of the rope with the round, prickly figure of Tomsk attached to it.

'Heeeeelp,' Tomsk wailed feebly. He too was suffering from air-swinging sickness.

'Hold on,' yelled Tobermory.

'I AM holding on,' replied Tomsk as he swung out of sight underneath the trolley.

With steady paws, Tobermory calmly adjusted the air valve. There was a gentle *Shuush* and the balloon shuddered slightly and began to grow thinner.

'They're coming down,' said Great Uncle Bulgaria.

'*Mille mercis*,' exclaimed Madame Cholet from behind the apron which she had thrown over her head, and she burst into tears.

'There, there, my good Womble,' said Great Uncle Bulgaria, 'don't distress yourself. What they'll want is a good hot breakfast. Of course, if you don't feel quite up to cooking . . .'

Madame Cholet wiped her eyes on the edge of the apron, sniffed and beckoned to Alderney and Shansi, who were clinging to each other like two small limpets.

'*Attention! Vite, vite*,' commanded Madame Cholet. 'We have work to do.'

'And I'll have a few words to say,' said Great Uncle Bulgaria under his breath. However, being a very wise old Womble, he held those words back until after the balloon had landed with the gentlest of bumps and its two, or rather one and a half occupants, had been escorted back to the burrow, and everyone had had two, if not more, helpings of everything.

'Exciting things often make one hungry. I've noticed it before,' said Orinoco to Bungo.

Great Uncle Bulgaria then said his few words.

'Yes, yes, I dare say,' agreed Tobermory absent-mindedly, as he wiped some fried grass crumbs off his moustache, 'but the first test flight is bound to throw up a few problems, you know.'

'It certainly threw me up!' said Tomsk, speaking for the first time in half an hour. 'Ho, ho, HO!'

Great Uncle Bulgaria's nose twitched. Alderney started to giggle. Wellington went, 'Heh, heh, heh. I say, Tomsk, sorry, but you looked just like a

30

pendulum on a clock.'

'A fat, furry pendulum . . .'

'Ho, ho, HOO.'

They laughed until their ribs hurt and the tears ran down their noses.

'I dunno,' said Tobermory as he wiped his eyes on his duster, 'if ever I saw such a lot of silly Wombles. And now, when I've made a few adjustments, I'll have everything airshape and ready for another flight tomorrow using Balloon Two. Only this time, I'll take someone IN the trolley with me. Who'll volunteer?'

And, much to their own astonishment, Orinoco, Bungo, Wellington and Tomsk all put their paws up together.

Wellington was the one chosen—because, as Tobermory tactfully put it, he was the lightest. Although he did mention to Great Uncle Bulgaria that there was another reason.

'Bright young Womble, Wellington. Dare say he'll grasp it all a bit faster. Nothing to it really, of course, but still . . .'

'You're sure it's going to be—well—all right, old friend?'

'Yes, yes. I've just invented the new self-releasing anchor. I'll show you how it works, if you like . . .'

'How very kind, Tobermory. Some other time perhaps. I'm due to give a little talk in the Womblegarten. I've entitled it "Who's Who in the Womble World." '

The self-releasing anchor worked perfectly and, after the first few nervous minutes, Wellington found that he was enjoying himself enormously, pointing out Queen's Mere, then King's Mere and

31

the Wimbledon tennis courts and . . .'

'I say, look, St Paul's and the Post Office Tower and Battersea Power Station and . . .'

'Yes, yes, yes. But now to work. This handle here, marked Prop One, is the first propeller . . .'

By the end of the second week, during which even Tomsk had learnt how to handle the balloon, those working down on the Common didn't even bother to glance up as the airborne Wombles swept overhead with just the faintest *tick-tick*-TOCK to announce their presence.

Down on the ground, matters were also proceeding smoothly, although Bungo was showing signs of getting rather above himself as he went round humming under his breath, '*Oh, those daring young Wombles in their flying balloons, they go up tiddy tiddy up, they go down tiddy tiddy down. Oh, those DARING . . .*'

Until even mild-mannered Cousin Botany was driven to say gently, 'Ah yes, up and down, up and down. It reminds me of my sailing-ship days, it does. Especially the Bay of Biscay. But, you know, *I* wasn't daring at all. Just the opposite. Scared out of my fur most of the time. My word. Now what did I come into the burrow for, I wonder? Do you think I can remember it?'

Bungo shuffled his back paws, scratched his ears and said in a very small voice, 'No, no, of course, you don't. Don't expect you to. I'll ask Great Uncle Bulgaria. He'll know . . .'

Cousin Botany shuffled off with his little eyes twinkling under the brim of his dreadful old hat, and Bungo returned silently to the Womblegarten where Miss Adelaide was waiting to give them their final Geography lesson.

'Well,' she said at the end, 'you haven't done too badly, I suppose.' Which was her way of saying she was proud of them. 'I have prepared for each of you a small set of map cards. These show all the known burrows. Those marked with three stars are the largest. The maps also depict the terrain—the type of countryside, Tomsk—and the prevailing winds. The cards fit into these little wallets, made by Shansi. The wallets in turn clip on to the belts sewn by Alderney. That is all I have to say at the moment. Yes, Cousin Botany?'

'Pardon me, Miss Adelaide,' said Cousin Botany from the doorway. 'I've just remembered why I'm here. I'm giving a talk on "Survival in Difficult Places", I believe.'

'Yes indeed. Would you allow me to stay and listen? I should be *most* interested to hear what you have to say.'

'Be my guest, Miss Adelaide. Now as you all know, my home country is Down Under. That is, Australia. Big country, Australia. Not too many cities, so if you do get into the Outback as we call it, you have to learn to fend for yourself. There *are* burrows, but they're few and far between because, of course, there's no great litter problem there. Although it may have changed a bit since my day, what with better roads and cars and trucks to drive on them.'

'Yes,' said Orinoco doubtfully, 'I expect there may be more clearing up to do now. But,' and he looked at his map card, 'Bungo and me . . .'

'Bungo and *I*,' corrected Miss Adelaide.

'Um. Yes. Well, *we're* going in the other direction, to America. So I don't quite see . . .'

'America is quite a big place too,' said Miss

33

Adelaide. 'Indeed, anywhere is a big place should you happen to get lost in the middle of it. Cousin Botany is about to explain what to do in such circumstances. Yes, Cousin Botany?'

'Ta, Miss Adelaide. First off then, if you *do* get lost, it's best to lie low during the day and to travel at night, because it's cooler and you have the stars to help guide you. If it's cloudy, you stick to your compass. Second, save your grub. That is, don't eat and drink *all* your provisions.'

'Oh dear,' groaned Orinoco, who had been wondering for some while if it was nearly supper-time yet. Now he felt more hungry than ever.

'Third, and maybe most important of all, don't panic and *stick together*. Fourth, try and work out at least roughly where you are and then make your plans. Fifth, watch the local animals. They'll know where there's water *and* food and some of them may be quite helpful if you treat 'em polite. Sixth, if the weather turns crook . . .'

'Mm?' said Tomsk.

'Unpleasant. Inclement,' said Miss Adelaide.

'Make yourself a shelter and sit it out. Seventh, good luck. Eighth, that's enough from me. Any questions?'

Both Wellington and Bungo had several, Orinoco was thinking only of food and Tomsk was slowly repeating everything he had just heard in a soft rumbling whisper. He rather hoped, in his heart of hearts, that perhaps he and Wellington might get lost, just once, because it sounded quite fun. He would like building shelters and travelling by night, not to mention tracking animals and birds.

'Mmmmm,' said Tomsk contentedly.

34

'My stomach's rumbling too,' agreed Orinoco. 'Oh, listen. The supper bell! Hurray!'

'Oh, and ninth,' said Cousin Botany, 'give my fondest regards to Great-great Aunt M. Murrumbidgee.'

'If we see her, yes of course we will,' said Wellington.

'You'll see her,' said Cousin Botany, 'she'll make very sure of that! Oh my word yes. Just you wait till you get to Australia, young Womble!'

CHAPTER 4

ONE, TWO, THREE, GO!

Quite suddenly the days seemed to rush past, until the date which Great Uncle Bulgaria had ringed in red on the calendar was only twenty-four hours away. The four volunteers had been given the whole day off to do exactly what they wanted. Orinoco spent most of his time having little naps and quite large snacks, since he was becoming increasingly anxious about how he was going to keep up his strength during the weeks that lay ahead.

Wellington would have liked to have given all his time to revision, but he was discovered sitting in the Womblegarten by Miss Adelaide, who didn't appear to understand Great Uncle Bulgaria's ruling that the travellers should do as *they* wished, for she only said, 'Enough is enough. Off you go into the fresh air.'

'But, Miss Adelaide, I'm going to get plenty of

fresh air for ages.'

'Not ages. Weeks. Off you go and do not argue.'
Wellington went.

'*There* you are!' said Tomsk. 'Been looking for
you everywhere. Come and have a run. Won't be
able to run sitting in a balloon all day.'

'That's true. I hadn't thought of that. OK,' said
Wellington, brightening up.

They trotted off, passing Orinoco as he was
dozing under a bramble bush with a large pile
of his favourite buttercup-and-daisy-spread
sandwiches beside him.

'Come and have a run,' puffed Wellington.

'Can't, having eighty winks,' said Orinoco and
reached for a sandwich.

Round the next bush they came upon Bungo,
who was standing as stiff as a poker with his fur all
up in prickles.

'Come and join us,' said Tomsk, running on the
spot. Bungo didn't answer. Tomsk ran round him
and reported back to Wellington. 'Got his eyes
closed. Looks very funny.' The two Wombles
circled their friend. He certainly did look
extremely odd.

'Sorry, but are you all right?' asked Wellington.
Bungo opened one eye, swallowed and then shook
his head.

'Got the colly-wombles,' he said huskily.

'If you . . . you mean you're scared—Ah-HEM—
nervous and all that, so am I,' said Wellington. 'So
is Orinoco—that's why he's eating so much. Bet
Tomsk is too, aren't you, Tomsk?'

'Mm,' said Tomsk, who hadn't really thought
about it much. 'Best thing for colly-wombles is
running. Come on.'

Bungo looked at his friends, sighed, swallowed and joined them. As they pounded past the burrow they could hear the distant 'chatter-chatter' of the Womblex machine in the Workshop.

'Tobermory's been getting dozens of messages from Wombles everywhere, saying they're looking forward to seeing us,' puffed Wellington. 'I must say it is rather an exciting adventure, isn't it?'

They glanced at each other, pushed each other and then thumped off across the Common with all their nervousness forgotten.

That evening, after supper, Great Uncle Bulgaria made (for him) a very, very, short speech.

'Good luck to our four young Wombles, Orinoco, Tomsk, Wellington and Bungo. We shall all be thinking of you and looking forward to your return and the many stories you will have to tell us.'

Everybody said 'Hear, hear' and 'Rather' and 'Good luck' and clapped and Great Uncle Bulgaria said, 'Bedtime. Tomorrow is a busy day.'

And that was that.

The morning was bright and chilly and there was a slight breeze as the two balloons, now delicately painted blue and grey so that they wouldn't show up too much against the sky, were inflated. The four young Wombles, fairly trembling with excitement, lined up and were checked first of all by Tobermory to make quite sure that they were wearing the right equipment. This was a zip-up jacket with four zip pockets apiece. Crash helmets. Belts with more pockets. Travel bags, which contained tools, a compass, pads and pencils and, in the case of Orinoco, three acorn buns. Then Madame Cholet checked their picnic bags which held delicious-looking packets of food and hot drinks. And finally, Great Uncle Bulgaria shook each of them by the hand, then looked at Tobermory who nodded.

'Right,' said Great Uncle Bulgaria briskly, 'off you go and behave yourselves. Remember—you are Wombles of Wimbledon.'

Orinoco and Bungo shook hands with Wellington and Tomsk. They then climbed into their two separate balloons and went through the take-off procedure.

'Start Prop One.'
'Start Prop One.'
'Start Prop Two.'
'Start Prop Two.'
'Set course.'
'Set course.'
'Let go anchor.'
'Let go anchor.'
'We have lift-off.'
'We have lift-off.'

And they had. Up and up and up went the two balloons, one moving to the left, the other to the right, and the only sound on the Common—apart from the first sleepy *cheep-cheep-cheeeep* of the birds—was a faint *clickety-click*-CLACK which slowly faded away as the balloons too seemed to disappear into the sky.

'Breakfast,' said Great Uncle Bulgaria loudly.

'I'll tell you what,' said Bungo.
'Breakfast?' said Orinoco hopefully.
'You've had breakfast.'
'Second breakfast, then.'

39

'No. I'll tell you what—this is fun. You'd better have first sleep and I'll carry on steering until it's your turn.'

'OK.'

Orinoco took a look at the green countryside far below, yawned, had a bit of a stretch and then wriggled into the neat little sleeping bag in the bottom of the trolley and in five seconds flat he was snoring happily. If this adventure was going to be just sitting, sleeping and eating perhaps it wasn't going to be too bad after all.

'*I'm a Womble of the Universe, a Womble of the skies*,' Bungo sang softly to himself. He had never felt so important in all his life before, and his fur fairly tingled with excitement as in the far distance he saw a faint, blue blur.

'Irish Channel,' said Bungo to Bungo, checking the instruments and then his first map card. 'A Woooomble of the Uniiiverse, de dum de dum de dum . . .'

However, even Bungo's enthusiasm began to flag after a while, as it's not much fun showing off for long periods if there is nobody to show off *to*. Besides which, all the excitement had begun to make him feel extremely hungry, so he carefully marked their position on the map, put the balloon on to automatic clockwork pilot and shook Orinoco.

'Whassamatta?' said Orinoco. 'Are we there?'

' 'Course not. Not for ages yet. It's second breakfast time.'

The two young Wombles opened up the packet marked 'Elevenses' and ate in silence until Orinoco, rubbing his stomach, remarked, 'All right, isn't it, this flying?'

'Bit boring. Once you've looked at one bit of sea all the rest looks the same. Just waves really. And a few boats.'

'Ah. Have another bracken bun; that'll cheer you up.'

Bungo shook his head and sniffed.

Orinoco looked at his friend and remembered that, after all, Bungo hadn't been a working Womble for all *that* long, and so he said in a voice which was really rather like Great Uncle Bulgaria's, 'Have a nap then. Do you good. Next to a nice bite of this or that there's nothing like a little forty winks to set you up.'

Which is how it came about that it was Orinoco, yawning and stretching and having an occasional hazelnut biscuit, who navigated the balloon for much of the journey; and even he began to feel a trifle restless until the moment when, through the haze, the coast of America was sighted.

'Cor,' said Orinoco, feeling absolutely wide awake for once.

'Cor,' echoed Bungo. 'Big, isn't it? EVER so big.'

They got out the binoculars and took it in turns to look through them, both of them talking at the same time as, thanks to Miss Adelaide, they recognised all kinds of places.

'What a lot of buildings,' said Bungo. 'Buildings everywhere! America must be covered in Human Beings. There don't seem to be many green bits . . .' And his voice shook nervously.

'It's just towns and things along the coast. There's a lot of green bits in the middle. Miss Adelaide showed us that on our maps and she's NEVER wrong, you know that. Or, when you are back in Wimbledon, are you going to tell her she

41

made a mistake?'

'No fear,' replied Bungo, cheering up. 'I wouldn't dare. I shouldn't think any Womble in the whole world has ever told Miss Adelaide she was wrong about anything! Well, I suppose we'd better check we're on the right course and all that.'

It was a great tribute to Tobermory's skill that Balloon One ever got anywhere, because hardly had Bungo spoken than everything about them seemed to vanish in a choking yellow fog.

'Smog!' said Orinoco. 'Masks, one, two, three, ON.'

The two Wombles pulled on the masks which the Womblegarten had made, and very strange it made them look, but neither of them noticed this, as quite suddenly ballooning stopped being fun and became rather serious.

'Automatic pilot,' snapped Orinoco.

'Automatic pilot,' echoed Bungo.

'Reading one, two, three.'

'Reading one, two, three.'

'On course.'

'On course. I say, Orinoco.'

'Shut up,' said Orinoco in a voice quite unlike his usually sleepy tones. 'We are going down. Release valve.'

'We are going down. Release valve. I say, Orinoco.'

'Shut UP. Fasten seat belts.'

Bungo gave Orinoco a hurt look from behind his mask and actually did as he was told without arguing.

There were a few moments of silence during which both Orinoco and Bungo held their breath and then there was a very faint bump as the trolley

42

hit the ground. Orinoco pushed up his mask and leant out carefully and looked down.

'We're there,' he said. 'It's the ground. We've landed. Cousin Yellowstone should be here any minute now.'

Bungo took a very deep breath and then said, 'I don't think he will be. You see, Orinoco, I hadn't, that is, I—er—well, I did sort of forget to reset the compass for landing. I did try to tell you. But . . .'

Orinoco shut his eyes very tight and counted up to ten and then to twenty and then to fifty.

'I'M EVER SO SORRY,' SAID BUNGO WAVERINGLY. AND QUITE SUDDENLY, HE WISHED MORE THAN ANYTHING ELSE IN THE WORLD THAT HE WASN'T A WOMBLE OF THE UNIVERSE OR EVEN A WOMBLE OF THE SKIES, BUT HOME AND SAFE ON WIMBLEDON COMMON. HE WOULD HAVE GIVEN ANYTHING AT THE MOMENT TO HAVE HEARD GREAT UNCLE BULGARIA TELLING HIM THAT BUNGO WAS A SILLY SORT OF NAME, BUT THAT IT SUITED *HIM*.

'You silly young Womble,' said Orinoco. 'Well, *what can't be put right makes a Womble sit tight.* [Old Womble saying.] We've travelled enough for now, so we'd better snuggle down here for a bit and make ourselves a nice little shelter like Cousin Botany told us to do. It's lucky we've got some food left or otherwise we'd have to start looking for animals to follow. Buffaloes and bisons and such. Have a bark-and-moss bun.'

'After I've made the shelter,' said Bungo who was feeling thoroughly subdued. *'I'll* do it. You sit tight.'

Orinoco gave him a sharp look out of his little round eyes and nodded. He remembered from some of his own past adventures that when you felt you'd made a bit of an idiot of yourself, it did help if you tried to do something useful.

Bungo took all the air out of the balloon and then draped it carefully over half the trolley, so that in a way it resembled a very small but cosy burrow; and then he climbed inside himself and the two of them ate half the last package of food and drank half of the last bottle of acorn juice. Then they snuggled down in their sleeping bags and within a couple of minutes they were snoring steadily, quite sure in their own minds that somehow Cousin Yellowstone would find them.

It was Bungo who woke up first and he did so with an awful start, because there was a hand over his mouth and a voice in his ear which was whispering, 'Don't make a sound. Lie quite still or else . . .'

Bungo whimpered softly, and did as he was told.

CHAPTER 4½

SILENCE

'Bulgaria,' said Tobermory, putting his grey head round the study door, 'are you awake?'

'Gerrumph. What? Yes, yes, of course I am,' replied Great Uncle Bulgaria, waking up with a jump which made his spectacles slide down his nose. 'What's the trouble? What's happened?'

Tobermory sat down and rubbed his ear with a screwdriver. In his other paw he held two pieces of paper.

'It's not what's happened,' he said, 'it's what *hasn't* happened, if you follow me. Well, first the good news and then the—er—other. This one's a message from Tante Lille in France and . . .'

'Charming, charming, Tante Lille, *tsk, tsk, tsk.* Dear me, I haven't seen her since the Paris Exhibition, in, now when was it? Eighteen hundred and . . . ah well, some time ago. I'm sorry, Tobermory, you were saying?'

45

'Tante Lille,' said Tobermory patiently, 'has sent a message on the Womblex to report that Wellington and Tomsk have arrived safely and that they are *très jolis*, whatever *that* means.'

'Jolly. Good.'

'Jolly good then. Funny way to describe 'em. And she goes on about Wellington working *très fort*, which I take it means he's writing down all their stories and that. And as for Tomsk, he's gymnasting *avec les petits* Wombles. Teaching 'em to do running on the spot and back-paw flips, I suppose. And that tomorrow, that is today now, they'll be off to . . .' Tobermory consulted the message again, 'meet Cousin Van Amsterdam. So that's all all right. Now then, about the other two, and that's where we run out of information. I had a Womblex earlier from Yellowstone saying that Orinoco and young Bungo had been sighted et cetera, et cetera . . . well, you know how Yellowstone runs on . . . and then nothing.'

'Nothing?'

'Nothing. Absolute silence. So I womblexed him back, but there was no reply apart from "Womblex now on clockwork automatic and will record your message. Proceed." Lot of nonsense. They should have a Womble standing by to take messages. Thought I'd better let you know.'

There was a long silence during which the two Wombles looked at each other. It was the kind of situation which both of them had feared, but had never mentioned. Great Uncle Bulgaria took off his spectacles and polished them and returned them to his nose.

'I think, Tobermory,' he said, 'we shall keep this to ourselves. Just pin the message from Tante Lille

46

on the board and the *first* message from
Yellowstone. Don't look so despondent, old friend.
If I know anything about Orinoco, he'll be all right.
And where Orinoco is, Bungo will be too. Have
you got anybody standing by the Womblex
machine?'

' 'Course I have. Little Shansi. You wouldn't
find me putting it on to automatic this, that and
the other. I've always said that machines are all
very well in their *way*, but that when it comes down
to it, nothing can replace Wombles. Besides which,
who wants to talk to a *machine*!'

Tobermory talked at some length and Great
Uncle Bulgaria nodded and went '*tsk, tsk, tsk,*'
every now and again, because he knew how
worried Tobermory was, but at the finish he only
said, 'Quite right, yes indeed. Well, if little Shansi
is on duty she will, I'm sure, be able to cope when
Yellowstone next calls us. So off you go,
Tobermory, and have a good sleep; otherwise you
won't be in a fit state to deal with what the morrow

47

will bring. And that, old friend, is an order!'

But after Tobermory had left the study, Great Uncle Bulgaria stopped being brisk and began to rock backwards and forwards in his chair. He was a great deal more anxious about Orinoco and Bungo than he had admitted. Had they got themselves into some dangerous situation? Why wasn't Cousin Yellowstone answering? What could have happened? And, if anything bad *had* occurred, then he, Great Uncle Bulgaria, was the one who was responsible.

Great Uncle Bulgaria shook his head, poured himself a hot acorn juice from the flask which Madame Cholet had left for him, drank it slowly and then quickly made his way to the Workshop where Shansi was sitting patiently in front of the Womblex machine, while she carefully unpicked a sweater which had been tidied up from the Common.

'Anything from Cousin Yellowstone?' asked Great Uncle Bulgaria.

Shansi folded her hands together and shook her head.

'I think I'll sit and wait with you for a while,' said Great Uncle Bulgaria.

CHAPTER 5

THE 'GINGERBREAD' BURROW

'There's a lot of trees about,' said Tomsk, 'miles and miles of trees.'

'Black Forest,' said Wellington, who was writing busily as he sat in the bottom of the trolley. Beside him were sheets and sheets of paper all covered in his neat, rather loopy handwriting.

'Doesn't *look* black. Looks green, like ordinary trees,' said Tomsk after a long pause. 'How do we land in trees, Wellington?'

Wellington put the top on his pen and got up and joined Tomsk who was steering. The view below them was certainly unusual, as there was nothing to be seen but the apparently endless forest, which undulated up and down like a great green sea.

'We don't land,' said Wellington briefly. 'Sorry, hang on while I look at our orders. Oh dear, our next meeting is with Onkel Bonn, so we must have gone a bit off course. Lend us a paw, Tomsk.'

'I wish we were going to Russia,' said Tomsk, as Wellington began doing sums on the back of his notes and then checking the dials and making adjustments. 'Do you remember Omsk who came under the wire from Kensington Gardens?'

' 'Course I do. A very large, silent sort of Womble. There, that should do it. Why?'

'Omsk wasn't silent really. Talked quite a bit. Told me a lot about the Wombles in Russia. Didn't understand all of it. But they did a lot of skiing and skating and going about in sledges. Trouble is,' said Tomsk and stopped dead.

Wellington looked at his large friend, who was standing first on one paw and then another in a fidgety way.

'The trouble is,' said Wellington, 'that you get jolly bored with just sitting in a trolley for hours on end.'

'Mm,' agreed Tomsk. 'It's OK for you, because you like writing things down and all that. But I do need to stretch my paws a bit. Used to it.'

Wellington looked at Tobermory's time sheet and then at the neat graph which he had been keeping. According to his reckoning, Balloon Two was just a bit ahead of schedule. Wellington did some sums in his head and for once in his life decided to behave recklessly. If Tomsk couldn't do a bit of running quite quickly he might get very itchy and restless indeed, and that could lead to something awful, like falling fur, which is bad for Wombles.

'We'll go down,' said Wellington, his own fur getting rather prickly as he spoke.

'But you said . . .'

'For a breather. Stand by for landing.'

'Stand by for landing, but Wellington . . .'

'Five, four, three . . .'

'Five, four, three . . .'

They landed gently in a small clearing. It was a charming place, with the early morning sunlight glinting through the tall trees and the grass splattered with small flowers which were just starting to unfurl their petals. A speckled thrush came hopping over to look at these strange visitors and the most beautiful red squirrel came chattering crossly down a tree.

'Isn't it smashing?' said Wellington softly.

'Not bad.'

Tomsk climbed out and did three somersaults and then two perfect back-paw flips. After which he started to rush up and down the clearing to get the itchy feeling out of his back paws, while Wellington put away his books and began to pick some of the flowers, grasses and ferns which he intended to press and take back to Wimbledon for the Womblegarten.

The tinkling sound of running water drew Wellington further down the clearing to where a small stream was muttering and chuckling to itself as it ran over brown stones, swirled in a little pool and then raced on again.

'It really is a beautiful place,' Wellington whispered and he dropped a leaf into the water and watched it go bouncing and dancing on its way. He shut his eyes for a moment, remembering some of the old fairy stories that Miss Adelaide used to read to him when he was a very small Womble in the Womblegarten. Why, he could almost imagine that any second Hansel and Gretel

51

would come wandering past, but if they did, then, of course, the Wicked Witch who lived in a gingerbread house would not be very far away . . .

Wellington opened his eyes with a shiver and looked down at his reflection in the pool, and then his fur really did stand up in prickles, for beside his own familiar face, he saw two other faces as well. Very, very slowly Wellington turned his head. Standing on either side of him were two, small, fluffy little Wombles, who were watching him with grave interest. One of them wore a little cap and an embroidered overall and had a wicker-work basket over her arm, while the other was wearing a funny sort of hat and shorts with coloured braces. He was carrying a long, pointed stick.

'How—how—how do you do?' said Wellington, stuttering for the first time in a long while.

The two strange Wombles bowed their heads politely.

'I say, excuse me, but,' said Wellington, remembering the *Burrows of the World* maps which Miss Adelaide had made, 'but are you lost?'

The two small Wombles shook their heads.

'But, but there's no Womble burrow marked here. You must be a long way from home. Mustn't you?'

The two small Wombles looked at each other and then at Wellington. They shook their heads.

'Talking to yourself again?' asked Tomsk, suddenly coming into view as he leapfrogged neatly over a tree stump. 'Oh, my word. Goodness. Whoops!' And Tomsk crash-landed out of sheer astonishment. The two small Wombles looked at Tomsk lying flat on his stomach with his eyes round as buttons and began to laugh. They

52

laughed so much they had to hold each other up, while the Wimbledon Wombles watched them in open-mouthed surprise.

'And what is going on here, please?' said a quiet voice.

The four young Wombles all stopped what they were doing and turned round. Standing under a tree was a very, very old Womble, leaning on a stick. He wore two pairs of spectacles, a hat with a tassel and an embroidered shawl and his fur was as white as snow. He looked even older than Great Uncle Bulgaria.

'You,' he said, pointing to Wellington, 'please explain yourself, mm?'

'I, we, that is, sorry, oh dear . . .'

'Mm. Where is your home burrow?'

'Wim-Wim-Wimbledon,' stuttered Wellington.

'*Ach*, really. Speyer, Heilbronn, pick up your stick and your basket. *Tsk, tsk, tsk,* such behaviour. Well, well. You must forgive their bad manners, but they are very young. And your names are?'

Wellington and Tomsk told him and the very old Womble nodded gently and asked, 'And, may I ask, what you are doing here, mm?'

Between the pair of them they managed to explain and at the finish the very old Womble nodded his head and said, 'If that isn't just like young Bulgaria Coburg. He always did have unusual ideas. Come, let me take you back to our burrow for some small hospitality before you once again set off on this adventure of yours. I find it all most amusing and interesting. Allow me to show you the way, mm?'

Wellington and Tomsk, keeping very close together, followed the very old Womble, while

53

Speyer and Heilbronn came last, whispering behind their paws.

The Black Forest Burrow was so well hidden that even Tomsk's sharp eyes didn't spot it, until the very old Womble knocked on what looked like the bottom of a fallen tree. The gnarled roots parted and an opening appeared, leading deep into a bank.

'Cor,' said Tomsk, while Wellington was past saying anything at this point. The burrow was lit by dozens of flickering candles in carved candlesticks. There were carvings and pictures everywhere and Wellington, who rather likes reading old history books, began to feel that he was stepping backwards in time. There were obviously no machines in this burrow, because even the Workshop had only benches and rack upon rack of hand tools.

'All handmade,' said the very old Womble, stroking a line of chisels which would have made Tobermory turn green with envy. 'You see, Wellington and Tomsk, we Wombles of the Black Forest have decided that here we can keep all the old crafts alive. If *we* don't do it, they may die away and become lost for ever. This is one of the oldest Womble burrows in the world. Very few Wombles even know that it still exists, which is why we are not marked on any of your maps. Mm?'

'Mm,' agreed Wellington.

'In the winter we are very quiet here, but during the spring, summer and autumn we have some tidying-up to do—although not very much.'

'Isn't it a bit dull?' asked Wellington.

'Oh no, not at all. Our young Wombles go off on expeditions to study wildlife and to draw pictures and collect all kinds of things. We specialise here in paw-craft and from their earliest years our small Wombles are taught a trade. Allow me to show you round the burrow.'

As it was early morning, and therefore by tradition in the Womble world tidying-up time— even if there was extremely little to tidy up—the burrow was nearly deserted. Which was just as well, as there was so much to see and take in without having to meet Wombles as well.

Every single room, even the Womblegarten, had the most beautiful furniture in it. There were tables with carved legs and highly-polished tops with lovely inlaid designs. There were chairs which ranged from little rockers to a most imposing throne-like affair which had Wombles carved all over the back and down the arms.

Wellington couldn't believe that this lovely furniture had been made from old bits and pieces, until he looked at the underneath of a pretty little stool and saw the letters ... YFFES BANANA stencilled on it. It made him feel quite homesick for a moment.

There were thick tufted mats on the polished, wooden floors, wonderful woodland paintings and Womble portraits on the walls. There were many highly-carved dressers, displaying painted plates and mugs, and heavily-embroidered curtains covered all the doors.

Finally they reached the kitchen where the cook, Frau Heidelberg, wearing the most wonderfully embroidered cap, apron and cuffs, had set out two steaming mugs of acorn juice, topped with thick daisy cream, and two enormous helpings of very rich-looking pudding which, she told the two by now speechless young Wombles, was her special fir-cone-and-moss strudel.

'Eat up, eat up,' she said. 'You are so thin for Wombles! Here we are getting much snow in the wintertime, so we have to eat to keep out the cold. Another helping? No? *Tsk, tsk, tsk.* I have heard so much of the fame of Madame Cholet, but perhaps she does not make strudel for you?'

By now both Tomsk and Wellington had realised that Frau Heidelberg answered her own questions, so they only shook their heads.

'*Tsk, tsk.* So I have taken the liberty of writing out the recipe for her, and together with it is this little wooden spoon which I feel she might like to have. Yes? It has the small Womble carved into the handle, which is nice. Mmm? More acorn juice? No! *Tsk, tsk, tsk.* Well, I hope you will come and visit us again at some time, but not during the winter when it snows. The snow often is more high than we are, so you would get lost. Now then, here are some little sandwiches, buns, rolls, chocolate and biscuits for your journey.'

And Frau Heidelberg handed over a large and bulging embroidered satchel, patted Wellington and Tomsk on the head, told them at least three times to give her fondest, best wishes to Madame Cholet and, in fact, was still talking as they thanked her and backed out of the kitchen. Her voice followed them down the passage to where the very old Womble was waiting for them by the front door. He, too, was holding a package which he gravely presented to Wellington with the words, 'I should like you to accept this small gift for young Bulgaria Coburg, which I present to him on behalf of the Wombles of the Black Forest. We are rather out of the world here and, having no Womblex machine, we of course knew nothing of the proposed *Vol. Ten*. However, I think this small gift may make one short chapter in the new modern History.'

Tomsk and Wellington bowed, said 'Thank you very much' and 'Rather' several times and were slowly and solemnly escorted back to the balloon, where Speyer and Heilbronn were waiting for them with their arms full of flowers and ferns as their parting gift. Everybody shook hands, lift-off procedure took place and the two Wimbledon Wombles rose up into the sky. They waved and waved until their Black Forest relations were out of sight, and then Wellington put the balloon on automatic and sat down. Tomsk was already sitting, with his legs straight out in front of him and a totally blank expression on his face.

'If it's that strudel whatsit that's worrying you, I've got a touch of colly-wombles myself,' said Wellington. 'Golly, what a burrow!'

'Mm,' said Tomsk, gently rubbing his stomach. 'Mm. Orinoco would have enjoyed that.'

'Mind you, I don't think I'd like to live there. There was too much of everything somehow and it was too quiet. I can't imagine those Wombles ever having a really good, noisy game of Wombles and Ladders . . .'

'Mm.'

Wellington looked anxiously at his silent friend.

'You're not going to be sick, are you?' he asked.

Tomsk roused himself slightly and shook his head. He tried to think of the words which would describe what he felt about the Black Forest Burrow. He settled on one.

'Cor,' said Tomsk. 'Cor!'

'Yes, I know what you mean. And I'll tell you something else, we never found out the name of that old, old Womble. He's so old, it didn't seem polite to ask somehow. Perhaps he's put his name on this present for Great Uncle Bulgaria. I'm sure it wouldn't matter if I unwrapped it and had a look.'

Wellington undid the paper and discovered the most beautifully bound book. Stamped on the front in gold letters were the words A Short History of the Black Forest Burrow.

And underneath this, Compiled and written by Hapsburg Von Hohenzollern Womble. 52 colour plates, 200 etchings.

Wellington got his breath back slowly. Thank goodness he hadn't known at the time that they were being entertained by one of the most illustrious and scholarly Wombles of all time. If he had known he wouldn't have been able to get out one word without stuttering. Wellington put the book back into its wrappings very, very carefully and reached for the small envelope marked 'Clover-root indigestion tablets.' He handed one to Tomsk and began to suck one himself.

'Cor,' Wellington said to no one in particular. 'Coo-er, cor!'

CHAPTER 6

YELLOW SKY AT NIGHT

['No Wombles' Delight'—American Womble saying]

It seemed to Bungo that several hours went past before the hand was removed from his mouth and he was able to breathe more or less properly again. More or less, because the air had rather a nasty taste to it.

'Don't move or make a sound,' the voice whispered. 'We find ourselves in a difficult situation territory-wise. Kindly inform your colleague of this.'

Bungo nodded violently and whispered in Orinoco's ear.

'Oi, *psst*, wake up, but please be quiet. I think we've been napped nabbed.'

Orinoco's eyes blinked open and he made a smacking noise with his tongue and did a bit of gentle scratching. He didn't seem to be very alarmed by this information, but then it takes a great deal to upset Orinoco, who is by nature extremely placid.

'Napped nabbed, nothing,' said the voice and out of the yellow murkiness above their heads emerged a strange figure. It was short and fat and distinctly round and wearing a shiny yellow coat, and an odd-looking hat, goggles and a mask.

'You two,' said this apparition, 'are the dirty laundry and I am about to take you to the laundromat. Hold still.'

Orinoco and Bungo looked at each other and Orinoco shrugged and patted Bungo on the shoulder. He didn't much care for being called 'dirty laundry', but on the other hand it didn't sound as if they were being napped nabbed. Orinoco reached for a biscuit, munched it as quietly as he could and slid back into his sleeping bag. Bungo remained sitting bolt upright.

There was a faint scuffling sound and the trolley appeared to be lifted slightly off the ground. Voices whispered softly, there was a squeaking noise and then the trolley jolted slightly and began to move bumpily forwards, lurching from side to side. A light flickered on somewhere close by, and in its beam they could see that the air was full of little yellow wisps of fog.

A voice called out something from a distance.

'OK, Mac, it's the laundromat,' was the reply.

The distant voice made a grumbling sound and a door was banged shut. The jolting went on and Orinoco actually dozed off, but Bungo continued to sit bolt upright with his eyes and his stomach going round and round. Suddenly they stopped moving and Bungo, his ears strained to catch every sound, realised that they were surrounded by whispering voices.

'Get 'em in back . . .'

'. . . steady . . .'

'One, two, three, we have lift-off . . .'

The trolley tilted alarmingly, was propelled up a small slope, then levelled out and came to a full stop. Something clicked shut and finally, most surprising of all, there was a soft *tick-tock, tick-tock, tick-tock*, and they were on the move again.

Bungo let out a small whimper and the strange voice whispered, 'Hold it. Not long now and we'll all be OK.'

The 'not long now' seemed to be rather an understatement, but finally the *tick-tocking* slowed down and then stopped, the trolley went rattling backwards down the slope and was bounced along the ground which suddenly became much smoother and there was a faint purring noise and a click.

'Well, well, well, and what do we have here?' said a deep voice.

Bungo, who had shut his eyes very tightly for the last five minutes, opened them reluctantly and looked up. The very next second he was out of the trolley and shivering with relief and excitement.

'It's you,' said Bungo. 'Oh, it's *you*.'

' 'Course it's me,' said Cousin Yellowstone, cuffing him gently round the head. 'Who else do you think it'd be? Huh? Come on, Orinoco, I know you're in there some place.'

Orinoco climbed out stiffly, politely hid a yawn and shook Cousin Yellowstone by the paw.

'Morning,' said Orinoco. 'Very nice to see you again. Been a long time. I take it we're in the right place?'

'Just about. But only just, which is largely thanks to young Idaho here. He was the one who rescued you.'

'Rescued?'

'Uh huh. Something must have gone wrong with your calculations, young Womble. You came down in the backyard of a motel.'

'It wasn't him, it was me,' said Bungo who was feeling quite faint from relief. 'I didn't do the sums right. Oh, I *am* glad to see you.'

'I'm sure it's mutual,' replied Cousin Yellowstone. 'I have to admit we were a little anxious when we lost contact with you. Things were rather busy hereabouts at the time, as we were on full Yellow Alert.'

'Full Yellow . . .'

'Smog. We had a lot of young Wombles out and about on their duties and they all had to be brought back fast. So we had them to worry over as well as you. It was a case of every Womble to his or her post. Even our cook, Ms Atlanta, had to abandon her stove.'

'Talking of which . . .' murmured Orinoco.

'You don't change,' said Cousin Yellowstone, starting to laugh. 'I guess that if you had to crashland in the middle of nowhere you'd think about food first.'

'Well, I wouldn't say that. Well, maybe . . .'

'Still, before we go along to the Wombletaria, let me introduce you to Idaho here.'

Idaho, a rather serious young Womble, had taken off his strange yellow clothes, goggles and mask and was now looking thoughtfully at his Wimbledon cousins. They all shook paws and Orinoco and Bungo thanked him for rescuing them.

'That's OK,' said Idaho. 'Sorry I had to call you dirty laundry, but it was too late in the day to say you were garbage and too early for you to be mail.'

'I don't care *what* you called us,' said Bungo, 'the important thing is that you got us out. It would have been awful if we'd woken up in the morning and found ourselves surrounded by Human Beings. I don't know what we'd have done. I say, this is a smashing burrow, isn't it, Orinoco?'

'Streamlined,' said Cousin Yellowstone. 'I'll take you on a tour round later on. But first the Wombletaria.'

As they had never heard of anything of that name before, Orinoco and Bungo didn't know what to expect; but their eyes were as round as they could be by the time they arrived there. They had never before seen a burrow like this, where everything was so neat and tidy and where lights flashed on and off in different colours at every corner.

'It's our communications system,' said Cousin Yellowstone. 'Just by looking at those lights a Womble can tell which storehouse has its full load of trash. It saves time and energy. Then, as I've already told you, all lights at yellow means full alert. That is, drop what you're doing and assemble in the main hall. If any one Womble in particular is needed, we flash his signal and he reports instantly to me. It's faster and more efficient than inter-burrow-telephone. Well, here we are.'

Orinoco looked round the Wombletaria and breathed deeply. Madame Cholet's kitchen was quite his favourite place in the Wimbledon burrow, but this was like at least four kitchens made into one. Instead of just one table, there were dozens of small ones, while at one end there was a long counter. To the side of this was a stack of small drawers, each with a card on the front of it.

Orinoco, like a Womble in a trance, read out what was printed on the cards, 'Daisy cream with hot grass sauce. Bracken buns and clover spread. Redwood triple-decker sandwiches. Toadstool takeaways. Moss crackers. Bluegrass-brunch . . .'

'That's our Eleven-taria,' said Cousin Yellowstone. 'Any working Womble who returns to the burrow for an early break helps himself—or herself—from there.'

'What a *very* good idea,' said Orinoco. 'I think I'll suggest it to Madame Cholet.'

'Well, bless me,' said a delighted voice. 'Are you talking of Madame Cholet? *The* Madame Cholet?'

And Ms Atlanta came hurrying into the Wombletaria with her front paws held out. She was wearing a very smart little white cap and a white overall which crackled as she walked. She held first Orinoco's paws and then Bungo's, as she went on, 'I am so glad and honoured to meet you. I've heard so much about you. I was meaning to come and greet you just the moment you arrived, but I had to go out on the Yellow Alert. Madame Cholet is just the best Womble cook in the whole world. Now do you have any recipes of hers that you could let me have? It would be just marvellous.'

Orinoco, with a speed which was remarkable in a Womble of his rather sleepy character, made a very quick decision.

'I think I *might* be able to help,' he said in a very serious voice, 'but that would mean spending a lot of time here in the—er—Wombletaria, you know.

64

So somebody else . . .' he glanced sideways at Bungo, 'would have to go out and about being brave and adventurous and taking notes for *Vol. Ten*. And I really don't think it's fair to ask . . .'

Bungo glanced at Idaho, who was watching him stolidly with his arms folded, and then at Cousin Yellowstone who was cleaning his spectacles on a large silk handkerchief.

'I think I could just about manage that,' said Bungo. 'I mean I like doing brave and adventurous things really.'

'That's settled then,' said Orinoco. 'Good. I say, Ms Atlanta, how about breakfast? I'm *starving*!'

'Coming right up,' said Ms Atlanta.

It really was a glorious meal and it was followed by a nice forty winks in a most luxurious dormitory, after which Orinoco made his way, without any help at all, to Ms Atlanta's cold store where she was deep-freezing all kinds of pies, casseroles, snacks, burgers and brunches.

'OK, let's go,' Bungo said to Idaho. 'I'll tell you what. I bet you don't have to pick up half as much rubbish as we do.'

'Rubbish?'

'Er—trash.'

'I'll tell you what. We do. Here just about everything is thrown away. But everything. We'll take the pickup truck, OK?'

'Yes, of course. OK, I mean.'

Bungo lost quite a bit of his bounce as Idaho led the way out of the burrow to where a small, clockwork van was waiting.

'This here is my pickup truck,' said Idaho. 'Last week I tidied up three washing-up machines, two iceboxes and four crates of trash.'

'Goodness,' said Bungo in a stunned voice. His biggest haul on Wimbledon Common had been three tidy-bags full of waste paper, tin cans and milk bottles in one day. Great Uncle Bulgaria had actually made a little speech about it and everybody had sung *For he's a jolly good Womble* after supper, and it had made Bungo feel very experienced and important at the time; but, compared with Idaho's tidying-up, it felt like nothing at all.

So Bungo didn't speak a word as they bounced away from the burrow, across the grass and finally to the edge of a very wide road on which cars and lorries were speeding along in both directions.

'The freeway,' said Idaho. 'Come dusk and they'll start dumping things in the back of the motels—just you see.'

'What's the biggest thing you've ever tidied up?' asked Bungo.

'Well,' said Idaho, leaning back and hooking his

66

front paws into his belt. 'I guess you could say it was a boat. Some Human Beings stopped their trailer up there by a motel and they had this boat joined on behind. They uncoupled it and just left it there among all the garbage. It wasn't that old either.'

Idaho's voice died away into silence, for at that very moment a larger car drew up over to their right, where there was a huddle of buildings. Joined to the back of the car was a trailer bearing a motorhome; to Bungo it looked like an entire house. Three Human Beings got out of the car, argued between themselves and then undid something between the car and the house and vanished on the far side of the house. The house began to rock backwards and forwards in a most alarming manner while Bungo and Idaho, who had drawn up in the shadows nearby, sat with their fur bristling.

Woomp, woomp, woomp.

'It's—it's going to come down on top of us!' whispered Idaho.

'Then let's get out of the way,' said Bungo.

But Idaho, like a Womble in a trance, could only stare up at the enormous shape which was teetering above them. His paws seemed to be frozen to the steering wheel.

'Oh dear, oh lor, oh me,' said Bungo and he pushed Idaho to one side and made a dive for the controls of the clockwork truck. Never having driven one before, he hadn't the slightest idea what did what as he pulled and pushed with all his might, with the result that there was the most awful grinding, scratching noise. Then the truck, instead of going forwards, jumped backwards and

67

then backwards again, rather like a reversing kangaroo. And not a moment too soon for, as the last jump took place, the house went *woooomp* and fell over on its side in a great shower of earth and dust.

Idaho and Bungo shook themselves violently, sneezed, had a good scratch and looked at each other.

'I'll tell you what,' said Bungo, 'we'd better join that house-thing up to this truck and take it back to the burrow. Funny things, Human Beings, throwing away a perfectly good house. I suppose they've got so many houses they don't know what to do with them. Come on.'

They spent a busy half-hour getting the house back on its wheels with the aid of the pickup crane. Then they coupled it on behind and set off very slowly back to the burrow. Idaho was rather silent, while Bungo whistled softly under his breath. He was feeling quite pleased with himself for the first time in several days, because, apart from anything else, he was busy working out the Womblex message which he hoped Cousin Yellowstone would send to Wimbledon. When it was finally sent it read:

ALL A-OK USA. YELLOW ALERT OVER. ORINOCO REORGANISING WOMBLETARIA. BUNGO HAS TIDIED-UP HOUSE. FONDEST PAW GREETINGS TO ALL. YELLOWSTONE!

CHAPTER 6½

SOMETHING AWFUL, DREADFUL AND HORRIBLE

'Tidied up a *what*?' said Great Uncle Bulgaria.

'The message reads "house",' said Tobermory doubtfully.

'Must have got it wrong. Not even Human Beings throw away *houses*. Still, the main thing is that they're safe and sound with Yellowstone. I don't mind telling you, Tobermory, I was a shade anxious about them.'

'Understandable,' said Tobermory, whose sharp eyes had seen the six empty mugs, which had once held hot acorn juice, ranged in a neat line near the Womblex machine. As Shansi had rather a sweet tooth and preferred drinking daisy mix through a straw, it hadn't been difficult to work out that Great Uncle Bulgaria had sat up all night, waiting for news. Added to which, the old Womble had deep shadows under his eyes, and his white fur had

69

lost its usual sheen.

'Well, now we know they're all safe and sound, we can take it easy for a bit,' said Tobermory. 'There's Wellington and Tomsk all nice and snug with Onkel Bonn—funny way to spell "Uncle" I must say—and with some mysterious news up their sleeves . . .'

'Yes, I can't help wondering what THAT is?'

'You'll just have to go on wondering until they get back and . . . oh hallo, Madame Cholet.'

'*Bonjour*,' said Madame Cholet, coming into the Workshop with a tray. She put the empty mugs on it and said quite severely for her, 'Now, Monsieur Bulgaria. I trust you will not let your clover juice get cold when I have made it with so much trouble. I've put it by your bed.'

'Clover juice! Bed! I'm not tired, Madame Cholet. And I have all my notes on our Wimbledon adventures to write out and . . .'

'Yes, indeed. However,' said Madame Cholet, opening the door with a deft kick, 'Alderney is practising her typewriting by doing the notes for you.'

'And then there is the list of working Wombles for tidying-up duty to make out,' said Great Uncle Bulgaria, trying to hide a gigantic yawn behind one white paw.

'Miss Adelaide's already done it. Indeed, I understand that even now she has the Womblegarten out on the Common. However, Monsieur Bulgaria, if you are only looking for excuses why you should not drink the clover juice which I have prepared for you so carefully, please say so.'

'Oh no, no, no,' said Great Uncle Bulgaria

hastily, 'quite the contrary. You make the most delicious clover juice in the whole world, Madame Cholet. In fact, I shall go and sample it at once.'

Great Uncle Bulgaria, who was practically asleep on his back paws, shuffled towards the door and then hesitated.

'You will call—er—come and tell me if there is any more news, won't you, Tobermory?'

' 'Course, Bulgaria.'

'Ah well, in that case. Goodni— I mean goodbye for the present,' said Great Uncle Bulgaria and off he went. The two Wombles who were left behind in the Workshop listened until they could no longer hear his shuffling footsteps and then Tobermory went, '*Tsk, tsk, tsk*. Tidied up a house indeed. "Mysterious news", I ask you!'

'*Tiens*,' agreed Madame Cholet, and returned to her kitchen.

At the same moment Alderney, who was feeling very important indeed, was sitting at Great Uncle Bulgaria's desk with a very large typewriter in front of her. She put a beautifully ironed piece of paper into it and looked carefully at Great Uncle Bulgaria's notes, which were propped up on the side of the desk. They were headed: *The Snow Womble*.

'Busy, yes?' asked Shansi quietly from the doorway.

'*Very* busy,' said Alderney. 'Got a lot of typewriting to do,' and down came her paws on the keys as she rattled out, *TeH sNow wOOmble*.

'Bother,' said Alderney and started again.

Up on the Common Miss Adelaide would very much have liked to say the same thing. But, as she did not approve of showing her displeasure, she

71

only remarked, 'Now then, Womblegarten, please be quiet and pay attention. At ONCE.'

The small Wombles, who had been playing leap-frog, catch-me-if-you-can, tag and hide-and-find, did as they were told. They lined up in front of Miss Adelaide with their little eyes shining and their soft fur covered with leaves and bits of bracken and pieces of grass.

'Stop shuffling and whispering,' said Miss Adelaide. 'Now, as it has been a nice day, a great many Human Beings will have been out walking and picnicking on the Common. Now, what does that mean?'

A very tubby little Womble put up his paw and said in a squeaky voice, 'Lots of rubbish, please, Miss Adelaide.'

'Correct. Only we say "a great deal of rubbish", not "lots of" which is bad grammar. So now we are going to tidy up that rubbish. Has everybody got their tidy-bag?'

'Yes.'

'Good. Now what do we do if we see a Human Being coming towards us?'

'Lie down flat and still and wait till they have gone away,' replied the Womblegarten in chorus.

'Correct. Follow me.'

It was a very pleasant evening as far as the Wombles were concerned, which meant that there was now a chilly nip in the air and a slight mist, so that not many Human Beings would be out on a night like this. As always, Miss Adelaide was quite right, for there was a great deal to be tidied up. Bus tickets, milk cartons, old newspapers, paper bags, any number of gloves, books, two cameras, one handbag, an umbrella, a great many tin cans,

72

seven plastic bags, a pair of gumboots, two watches, nine golf balls, three kites, a supermarket trolley, one pram with pram rug, eleven ballpoint pens and a bowler hat.

'Dear, dear me,' said Miss Adelaide as the Womblegarten moved down the long slope from the Windmill towards the trees. 'I do believe that, as from tomorrow, I shall have to provide larger tidy-bags.'

She clapped her front paws together and was about to recall the Womblegarten, as it was nearly their suppertime, when the tubby little Womble came running up to her and said breathlessly, 'Miss Adelaide, something awful, dreadful and horrible has happened!'

Miss Adelaide felt her grey fur go spiky with worry, but she only said calmly, 'Please show me to what you are referring. Everybody come here.'

A thin moon was rising through the mist as they made their way down the slope and into the bushes.

'There,' said the tubby little Womble in a whisper. 'Something awful, dreadful . . .'

'That's enough of that. All of you wait here,' said Miss Adelaide and, using the umbrella which she had tidied up, she parted the bushes and moved forward into the darkness. For a moment she couldn't hear or see anything and then she became aware of a heavy, distressed, panting sound and her sharp eyes picked out a flash of white and black.

'Dear, dear me,' said Miss Adelaide calmly, 'are you in trouble?'

There was a deep grunt which sounded rather like *Gmmmmmmmm*.

73

'Will you allow me to look?'

Gmmmmmmmm.

'Quite so.'

The Womblegarten, who were now all clinging together, swallowed and whimpered softly as Miss Adelaide appeared to vanish into the darkness of the bushes. However, their fur began to lie down a little as they heard Miss Adelaide's voice talking gently but firmly, interspersed with a *gmmmmmmmm*. Then, quite suddenly, there was a distinct *'Yooooow!'*, at which everybody's fur turned into prickles again.

'Most unfortunate,' said Miss Adelaide, re-appearing in the moonlight. 'Please bring me that pram. Furthermore, I need two helpers. You and you, forward please.'

The tubby little Womble and his best friend gulped and then did as they were told. After all, with Miss Adelaide there, nothing too awful, dreadful and horrible could happen.

'Poor creature,' said Miss Adelaide from the black shadows of the bushes. 'Do you see how he had been putting out all his bedding for a nice spring-cleaning, and then he got his paw caught in this very nasty can. Now when I say "one, two, three, lift", you will both do exactly that. Are you ready? One, two, three . . . LIFT.'

There was a lot of heavy breathing, a frantic howl and then out of the darkness appeared Miss Adelaide, her two helpers and the pram. Lying in the pram was something large and furry and black and white with two gleaming, rather cross eyes.

'Womblegarten,' said Miss Adelaide, 'pay your respects to poor Mr Badger.'

The Womblegarten, letting out an enormous

74

sigh of relief, did exactly as they were told.

'We will now take Mr Badger to the Chief Ranger's house,' said Miss Adelaide. 'The Chief Ranger, even if he *is* a Human Being, will know how to get this nasty tin can off Mr Badger's paw. Right, one, two and quick sharp.'

Ten minutes later, the Chief Ranger heard a loud knock on his front door and went to open it. In the shaft of light from his office, he saw a very battered child's pram and tucked inside it, under a tattered blanket, a very angry badger with a large and jagged tin can trapped round its fore paw.

'Well . . .' said the Chief Ranger. 'Well, that is, how did you, dear me, I'll have that can off you in a jiffy, but how did . . .'

'*Grrrrrrrr,*' said the badger, blinking his little eyes and bristling, because he is a very, very, shy animal, and he strongly dislikes having to have any dealings with Human Beings. However, there are times when even badgers have to accept help and ten minutes later with a neat bandage round his paw, he was travelling heavily back towards his home.

The Chief Ranger watched him vanish into the darkness and then for the first time he looked more closely at the old pram. Attached to it was a small piece of paper. WITH THE COMPLIMENTS OF THE WOMBLEGARTEN.

'*Tsk, tsk, tsk,*' said the Chief Ranger and went back to his desk.

Once they were home and safe in the burrow, every member of the Womblegarten began whispering, pushing and shoving as they got into line and then trooped off to the Workshop with their tidy-bags.

'My word,' said Tobermory, 'you have done well. All those ballpoint pens, just when we needed them too, *and* a supermarket trolley, assorted gloves . . .'

Shansi, who was standing to one side of Tobermory, scribbled carefully in her notebook as Tobermory sorted everything out.

'Newspapers, various—and yes a copy of today's *Times*, well done,' intoned Tobermory. 'Fifteen milk cartons; put 'em to one side, Shansi, for Cousin Botany—bus tickets; they'd better go for pulping and—oh sorry, Miss Adelaide, I didn't see you for a moment. Well, your Womblegarten *has* done you proud.'

'Yes, indeed,' agreed Miss Adelaide. 'It's been a most instructive evening. I wonder if you would be good enough to let me have some nice clean ironed paper bags early tomorrow for classes one and two.'

' 'Course, Miss Adelaide. Might I—er—ask what for, exactly?'

Miss Adelaide removed her spectacles and polished them before looking proudly at her young Wombles.

'We are going to write an essay,' she said, 'on some aspects of the wildlife of Wimbledon Common. The essays will be entitled *The Rescuing of Mr Badger*. And the best of the essays will, I am certain, be reprinted as a small chapter in *Vol. Ten* of our History. Goodnight, Tobermory.'

' 'Night, Miss Adelaide.'

Tobermory scratched behind his ear with a screwdriver and glanced at Shansi.

'Now what do you suppose Miss Adelaide meant by that?' he asked.

76

'Cannot say,' replied Shansi, 'but am sure that whatever Miss Adelaide says will happen, will happen. Miss Adelaide always right.'

(She was perfectly correct. One chapter in *The Womble History of the World, Vol. Ten* is called *The Rescuing of Mr Badger*. Subtitle: *Something awful, dreadful and horrible.*)

'Never mind that now,' said Tobermory, 'there goes that Womblex machine again. *Tsk, tsk, tsk.* Come along, Shansi, and don't dawdle!'

CHAPTER 7

LOST . . .

Wellington woke out of a light sleep and shivered violently. He was wearing his zip-up jacket and hood, boots, mittens and an enormous blue scarf which had been a parting present from Onkel Bonn (he had turned out to be a very stout, jolly Womble who kept going 'ho, ho, ho' all the time) and, of course, he had his own nice thick fur. So altogether he should have been very warm and cosy indeed. But he wasn't. He was distinctly chilly.

Wellington grunted softly to himself, rubbed the end of his nose and got to his feet. He had got so used to being airborne that he could now move about the trolley without making it sway at all. In fact, when he and Tomsk did touch down at their various burrows of call, they often felt as if the solid ground under their feet was moving about. So now he stepped neatly over the snoring figure of Tomsk and went to inspect the automatic pilot. It was set firm and the propellors were making their usual steady *tick*-TOCKing sound but, in spite of these reassuring facts, Wellington sensed that something, somehow, was wrong.

'Can't understand it,' Wellington muttered to himself and he checked the controls again. His spectacles seemed to be getting misty, so he took them off, blew on them and cleaned them carefully on the end of the blue scarf. The strange thing was that they began to get cloudy again almost immediately, so he pushed them down to the end of his nose and looked over the top of them. It was a very dark night indeed, with a few stars glittering directly overhead, while to left and right there was just a white haze.

'Quite pretty, really,' said Wellington, his breath making little white puffy clouds. 'But v-v-very c-c-cold. And it shouldn't b-b-be as c-c-cold as this on our route. Atishoooo!'

'Whassat?' said Tomsk, sitting up in his sleeping bag. 'Oh, it's you, W-W-Wellington. I say, how about some h-h-hot bracken choc-choc . . . *brrrr*. OH!'

Wellington also said 'Oh!' at the same moment, for, quite suddenly, the white haze all around them stopped being clouds and became very solid-looking indeed.

'Snow,' said Tomsk in a pleased voice. 'I say, Wellington, just look at all that snow. Is this Russia?'

'No. Yes. It c-c-can't be. Not unless we're going in the wrong direction. And we can't be doing that because . . .' said Wellington and stopped suddenly. He bent forward and took a really close look at the controls. They were set hard all right—

they were covered in ice!

'More snow, look,' said Tomsk, sliding out of his sleeping bag and throwing his arms backwards and forwards across his chest. 'That's just about the most snow I've ever seen.'

Tomsk and Wellington stood side by side in awestruck silence, as an enormous mass of white drifted past them. It seemed to climb right up into the sky.

'It's big,' said Tomsk, almost tilting over backwards. 'Bigger even than all of Wimbledon Common. What is it, Wellington?'

'A m-m-mountain,' said Wellington, his teeth chattering. 'And there are lots of them. Look.'

As Wombles can see very well in the dark, they had no difficulty in making out they were now travelling along a kind of aerial valley between these vast, snow-covered giants.

'I like snow,' said Tomsk slowly, 'but do you think we're in the r-r-right place, Wellington?'

Wellington shook his head. He felt very small, very lost and extremely frightened. According to Tobermory's flight plan they should by now be reaching much warmer weather as they ballooned towards Australia. But what even Tobermory had been unable to anticipate was that the weather was not behaving as it should have done, and that there were all kinds of unexpected crosswinds blowing about and that air pressure was all over the place.

It might have been of some comfort to Wellington and Tomsk to know that at this particular moment Wimbledon Common, which should have been blossoming with spring flowers, was itself under a foot of snow; while Orinoco and Bungo, who had been told quite firmly by Cousin

Yellowstone that they had better wrap up against a nip in the air, were, in fact, gasping in the middle of a heatwave. All *they* knew was that they were totally lost in very nasty surroundings.

'It's definitely not the right place,' said Wellington in a rather wobbly voice. 'I don't even know what place it is. Oh dear. Sorry.'

'Nothing to be sorry about. Not your fault,' said Tomsk fairly. 'Not anybody's fault. The control box thing has got ice all over it. So it's not even *its* fault. Wonder where we are, though. *Brrr*. Let's have some hot choc-choc-choc . . .'

Tomsk blew on his front paws, making an absolute cloud of steam, and undid a flask. He took a deep swallow, gulped and gave the flask to Wellington.

'Wherever we are it's not bad,' said Tomsk, slapping his paws as he tried to think of the right word to describe the gigantic mountains. 'Sort of big.'

'Mm,' agreed Wellington. He swallowed the last of the hot bracken chocolate and felt a little braver, but not much. There didn't seem anything much they could do, but just hope that, iced-up or not, the automatic pilot would get them out of this silent, freezing world of mountain after mountain. Unfortunately, Balloon Two also did not like the cold and it soon became obvious that, whether they liked it or not, they were starting to sink towards those great white slopes.

'Oh dear,' whispered Wellington.

'Mmmm,' agreed Tomsk.

They both held their breath as the trolley narrowly missed a jagged, snow-covered crag and then, as though at its last gasp, the balloon gave a

81

soft hiss, lurched and descended gently on to a slope. The trolley tilted slightly and then righted itself, while the propellors bit into the snow, sent up a small flurry of flakes and stopped.

'No bones broken,' said Tomsk. 'Now what?'

'I don't know,' said Wellington. 'Oh dear, oh dear, OH DEAR.'

'No good making a fuss. Better eat something. Eating makes you warmer.'

The two Wombles, perched on the edge of nowhere, blew on their front paws and then opened their last but one packet of food. As this had been supplied by Onkel Bonn's burrow, it was pumpernickel fruit cake and Deutschenessel [German nettle.]. Both of which, luckily, are full of vitamins as well as being warming and delicious.

'Perhaps it'll get less cold when the sun comes up,' said Wellington, looking at the inky darkness.

'Mmmm,' said Tomsk doubtfully. He sighed as he remembered how he had once hoped that they might get lost, so that they could build a shelter and watch out for wild animals and altogether have a nice, interesting adventure. The difficulty was that there was nothing to make a shelter out of, and there were certainly no animals up here in this silent, shimmering, white world.

Tomsk glanced at Wellington and thought deeply. Clever sort of Womble, Wellington. Good at reading books and having ideas and inventing things, but at the moment he was just sitting there and shivering. Well, perhaps he, Tomsk, had better do something.

'Tell you what,' said Tomsk, 'we'll make a snow burrow. Plenty of snow about. Come on.'

Tomsk climbed out of the trolley, fell flat on his

82

face, got up and began to gather armfuls of snow.
He'd always liked the cold weather ever since he
had taught himself to ski, and after a few minutes
he began to enjoy himself as he patted the snow
into shape.

'Going to make a shelter, going to make a
burrow,' Tomsk sang in his rumbling voice. 'Come
on, Wellington, lend us a paw.'

But Wellington just sat in the trolley, staring at
the ice on the controls and listening to the shrill
cry of the wind. He felt as if he couldn't move—in
fact, as if he'd never move again, but would just sit
here for ever and ever, staring at nothing but the
whiteness of the snow. He might even drift off to
sleep in spite of being so cold. His head nodded
forward and his eyes blinked shut and he was more
than three parts asleep when Tomsk's voice
rumbled in his ear, 'Come on, nearly there. We've
got a lovely burrow all of our own. Have a look.'

And Wellington was lifted by the scruff of his

neck out of the trolley. Tomsk shook him gently, till Wellington's eyes blinked open a couple of times and then widened in real astonishment, for there, on the side of the icy mountain and in the middle of nowhere, was a small snow burrow. It was even furnished with their sleeping bags and belongings, and altogether it looked quite homely and even warm and welcoming.

'Oh,' said Wellington. 'I s-s-say. S-s-sorry. Oh, Tomsk.'

'Not bad, is it,' agreed Tomsk. 'Home from home. Let's have a grass bread sandwich and a cupful of acorn juice. *I* rather like it here, you know. Quiet.'

They munched and drank in silence, hardly aware of the shrill wind outside because it was remarkably cosy in their snow burrow.

'G'night,' said Tomsk, zipping himself into his sleeping bag. 'Things'll look better in the morning, you know.'

'Yes,' agreed Wellington, 'and Tomsk, I'm sorry about . . . that is . . . I should have helped . . . oh dear . . .'

'Zzzzz,' was the answer.

'Yes,' said Wellington and, remarkably, in the middle of nowhere, he too was going 'zzzzz' within a matter of seconds.

Indeed, it seemed only seconds later that both of them were suddenly awakened by the sound of deep, rumbling voices.

'Whassat?' said Wellington and Tomsk together.

The voices stopped and there was absolute silence apart from the wind. Wellington and Tomsk sat up, stretched, yawned and looked at each other and then at the front door of their snow

84

burrow.

'Better have a look,' whispered Tomsk. 'You stay there.'

Tomsk wriggled out of his sleeping bag and crawled on all fours out of the snow burrow. Then he straightened up and looked around, blinking. It was broad daylight now and, for a moment or two, he couldn't see anything at all because the snow was absolutely blinding white and it was like trying to look directly at the sun. So Tomsk put his knuckles into his eyes and rubbed them and tried again. He looked up and down and left and right, went *gmmmm* deep in his throat, took three big breaths and dived back into the burrow.

'It's, it's . . . haaaaaaar,' said Tomsk and pointed.

Wellington started at him, wondering for a moment if his friend was suffering from Mountain Madness, and then decided to see for himself. He shuffled cautiously out of the burrow on his knees, blinked, knuckled his eyes and went 'Haaaaar'.

'Do you see, what I see?' whispered Tomsk.

Wellington nodded violently.

The two young Wombles from Wimbledon got up off their knees and looked left and right and then up and down. They didn't make a sound, because they couldn't think of anything at all to say. Which was hardly surprising, because standing in front of them were four absolutely gigantic snow-white Wombles.

Very slowly and with great dignity one of them stepped forward, put his front paws together and bowed.

'Haaaaah,' he said.

'Heeeeeh, um haaaaaah,' said Wellington in a

rather high voice which changed key halfway through. He bowed solemnly and kicked Tomsk to do the same.

'Ooooooh,' said Tomsk.

'You are Womble?' asked the enormous snow-white creature.

'We are Womble. Sorry. Yes, we are Wombles, you know. I say!'

'No, I say. Welcome. We are honoured. We too are Wombles. Haaaaah.'

'Haaaaah,' agreed Wellington, bowing and nodding.

'Haaaaah. Coo-er,' agreed Tomsk.

'Fine burrow,' said the enormous Womble. 'Not as fine as ours. But fine.'

'Ta,' said Tomsk, who felt that something was called for at this point.

'You stay here with us in mountains?'

'No fear. I mean, sorry, um, we have to travel on, you know. Only we're a bit stuck.'

'Stuck?'

'Er,' Wellington glanced desperately at Tomsk, who was staring up at his enormous cousins with his mouth open, 'er, our balloon . . . balloon?'

Wellington pointed desperately to the limp balloon, which was lying on the very edge of the mountain, and drew a round shape in the air. The enormous Womble watched him gravely, and then, most surprisingly and very like Onkel Bonn, went 'Ho, ho, HO' in a great rumbling voice which made some of the snow slide down the mountain.

'Should be round, yes?' he roared. 'So you go up into the sky. Um?'

'UM. Yes,' agreed Wellington and, because he suddenly felt happy and not frightened and worried any more, he went 'Ho, ho, ho.'

'Ho, ho, ho,' echoed Tomsk.

'Yes. Good. We will make it round,' said the enormous Womble. 'But not until the sun comes up again. Until then, you come back to our burrow and have food and hot drink and talk to us. Yes?'

'Yes. Rather,' said Wellington and Tomsk, and Wellington added, 'I say, sorry, but I haven't introduced us. I'm Wellington, you know, and this is Tomsk and we're from the Womble burrow under Wimbledon Common in England. We're on our way to Australia, only we seem to have got a bit lost. In fact, we don't know where we are. Sorry. But what is this country?'

The four enormous snow-white Wombles looked at each other and then rumbled with laughter, and then the one who had done all the talking stepped forward and bowed and said, 'Welcome to our country, Wimbledon Wombles of England. We are your very long-lost cousins. We are the Great White Wombles—of Tibet.'

'Well, I never,' said Wellington. 'I say, just *wait* until Great Uncle Bulgaria hears about this!'

CHAPTER 8

. . . AND FOUND

As it soon became obvious that even Tomsk had not got a hope of keeping up with their enormous white cousins, there was a brief discussion which ended with the two Wimbledon Wombles being given piggybacks. They hung on tightly to the extremely thick and rather long white fur, and soon discovered that this was the ideal way to travel in the mountains. For one thing they were protected from the bitter winds and, for another, the Tibetan Wombles moved in a curious gliding manner. They took enormous running leaps, their great paws hardly seeming to touch the snow at all when they did land. Even the Great White Womble carrying the trolley didn't seem to be bothered by its size and weight, but just handled it as if it was a largish tidy-bag.

Tomsk was blissfully happy, for this was just the kind of adventure he liked; and he began to hum tunelessly in the back of his throat as they seemed to fly over the glittering snow. But Wellington, who is by nature very curious about everything, was puzzled about the behaviour of the fourth White Womble. He was in charge of the balloon but, instead of carrying it in his arms, he was leaping along and dragging it behind him. Wellington would very much have liked to ask why, but he didn't quite like to. At least not yet. So instead he tried to work out just how big these gigantic running strides were.

'Crumbs, about forty feet,' Wellington whispered to himself. 'It must be a world record. That'll be something to put in *Vol. Ten!*'

They glided into a deep, blue shadow and then, out of nowhere or so it seemed, they saw before them a dark, indigo shape which turned out to be an enormous front door. Although it appeared to be made of solid white rock and was extremely big, it opened like a drawbridge in the traditional Womble way.

'Welcome to our humble burrow,' rumbled the Womble who was carrying Tomsk.

'Thanks very much,' said Wellington politely.

He had never seen such a grand and enormous burrow before. Carved out of the side of the mountain, it had a great arched roof; and the entrance hall alone would have housed the entire Wimbledon burrow with room to spare. It was lit by enormous globes and hanging all round the walls were thick, silky-looking rugs, woven with glowing colours. There didn't seem to be much furniture and what there was, was made of simple, highly polished wood.

Standing to one side was a brass gong which was

at least six feet across, and when one of the Wombles hit it, it went 'BOOOOOOOM-*nnnnnnng.*'

'Dear me,' said Wellington, who was running out of words.

'That is to let Dalai Gartok know that we have arrived. He was expecting you and is looking forward to the meeting.'

'Expecting *us*?' said Wellington. 'But how did he know we were coming?'

'Dalai Gartok knows everything . . .'

'And the answer to it, just like Great Uncle Bulgaria,' said Tomsk, who already felt thoroughly at home. 'Smashing burrow you've got here.'

'Ta,' said the big White Womble, trying out this useful word for the first time. 'This way.'

Dalai Gartok was sitting in a room which was about four times the size of Great Uncle Bulgaria's study but, nevertheless, it somehow looked very similar. There were dozens of bookshelves, a map of the world, a great desk made of stone and covered with more books and papers, and what appeared to be a speaking tube carved out of wood and a thick, silky carpet on the floor. Added to which, Dalai Gartok was sitting in a massive rocking chair.

It was difficult to make out how old he was as, naturally, like all the other Tibetan Wombles, his fur was snow-white. Nor did he wear spectacles, but on his head was a yellow skullcap, while a beautiful yellow shawl was draped round his shoulders.

He put down the quill pen he had been using, and beckoned to Wellington and Tomsk to come closer. They did so a little nervously, until they saw that his eyes were very kind, extremely wise and held a distinct twinkle.

'So,' he said, 'you will be Wellington and you Tomsk. Please sit down. I have been very much looking forward to making your acquaintance.'

'Thank you. Us too. Sorry, I mean we're very pleased as well.'

'Mm,' agreed Tomsk.

'Good. You will join me in some yellow-flower tea and lichen cakes?' Dalai Gartok picked up the speaking tube and spoke into it softly.

'Rather,' said Wellington and Tomsk together, as they suddenly realised that they were absolutely starving hungry.

Must be the mountain air, Wellington thought to himself and at the same moment he knew for certain that Dalai Gartok had seen what was in his mind. It made his fur go a bit prickly and Dalai Gartok said softly, 'I apologise and will endeavour not to do that again. Let me answer your next question before you think of it. How did I know you were coming? It is very simple. I have been aware that you were approaching for some time. I have always lived in the mountains, and when you get to my age you have the fortunate gift of listening to what they and the wind have to say. In the times in which we now live it is a most useful gift, since we can anticipate when the next group of Human Beings will arrive. There are so many of them too!'

'Human Beings, *here!*' said Wellington.

'Yes, indeed. Ah, the tea and cakes, thank you, Cousin One.'

The large White Womble, who had piggy-backed Tomsk, came in with an enormous tray and put it down on the desk. Then he bowed deeply,

91

winked at the young Wombles and walked out backwards.

Dalai Gartok poured out the tea, which was hot, very thick and had a somewhat strange taste, and then passed round the lichen cakes which also had a distinctive tang and looked like little pies. Tomsk had six and Wellington five.

'The Human Beings come to climb the mountains,' went on Dalai Gartok. 'They come from all over the world to do so, and in their clumsy way they do it quite well. But they bring so much equipment with them and they leave a great deal of it behind. It never ceases to astonish me how wasteful they are. Tents, oxygen masks, stoves, sleeping bags. And so on and so on. *Tsk, tsk, tsk.*'

'*Tsk, tsk, tsk,*' Wellington and Tomsk agreed politely, if rather thickly, through the lichen pies.

'When I was young,' said Dalai Gartok, rolling the tiny cup of yellow-flower tea between his large white paws, 'there were hardly any Human Beings here at all. It was very peaceful. However, I depart from the point. I am so pleased that Cousins One, Two, Three and Four found you quite quickly. I was anxious about your safety, but it was a needless anxiety. I should have known that Young Bulgaria would have trained you well.'

'Do you know Great Uncle Bulgaria?' asked Tomsk. 'He never told us about you.'

'I don't know him. I know *of* him. There was a certain Yellowstone Womble who passed through India quite recently, some eighty or ninety years ago. He met and talked with Quetta Womble and word came back to me. It always does. I trust you will give Young Bulgaria my regards and sincere

92

best wishes.'

' 'Course,' said Tomsk.

'Good. However,' and Dalai Gartok put down his cup and shut his eyes, 'I would prefer it if there is only the smallest reference to us in *Vol.*—er—yes, *Ten* of *The Womble History of the World* which you Wimbledon Wombles are compiling. You see, we prefer to remain rather quiet.'

'Yes, of course. We'll tell—um—Great Uncle Bulgaria as he is now. But, sorry, could I ask why?' said Wellington.

'I should be very surprised if you didn't,' said Dalai Gartok, opening his eyes and helping himself to another cup of tea. 'The reason is, Wellington, that recently (by which I mean during the last century or so) there has been far too much interest about us in the Human world. We are quiet, orderly and peaceful by nature, as are all Wombles; but, because we have chosen to live up in the mountains minding our own business, certain stories about us have been told. If we leave so much as one pawmark in the snow all kinds of Human Beings suddenly appear. They take photographs and they write a great deal of nonsense about us. They even try to track us down and take us prisoner. It's ridiculous, upsetting and undignified.'

'It's the same on Wimbledon Common,' said Tomsk. 'Never leave you alone, Human Beings. I say, could I have just one more pie? Ta.'

'I'm sure Great Uncle Bulgaria would understand,' said Wellington, passing his cup across for some yellow-flower tea. It was really very tasty once you got used to it.

'Good, good,' Dalai Gartok crossed his great

white paws and bowed. His eyes twinkled more than ever as he went on, 'Now you have had your—er—elevenses—and before you have a proper lunch, I am sure you would like to see round the rest of our humble burrow.'

'That was only "elevenses"?' said Tomsk. 'Cor, wouldn't Orinoco like it here!'

'Orinoco,' said Dalai Gartok softly, 'now let me see. He would be travelling with small Bungo, I think. Would you care to know what is happening to them?'

Wellington and Tomsk looked at each other and then at the Great White Womble, who once again shut his eyes, folded his arms and became very still.

'It's better than the Womblex, eh?' said Tomsk in a whisper.

'Shut up,' replied Wellington.

'*Tsk, tsk, tsk,*' said Dalai Gartok, suddenly waking up. 'The sun shines very brightly on them. Too brightly. Even Orinoco, who appears to be rather fat, has lost his appetite and is asking for iced clover-root juice. Small Bungo is eating a moss-cream sundae.'

'Is anybody saying anything?' asked Wellington.

'Yes, Yellowstone is speaking all the time.'

'Sounds like him,' said Tomsk. 'What about Wimbledon, please?'

The old Womble went quiet again and then actually chuckled.

'Bulgaria is at his desk writing, Tobermory is in his Workshop and looking very worried and Madame Cholet, who I believe is supposed to be the best Womble cook in the whole world, is very busy in her kitchen. The burrow is full of activity and there are a great many very small Wombles hurrying in all directions. They are holding little packets. I am sorry, the picture fades . . .'

'The Womblegarten,' said Wellington, 'going off on tidying-up work, I expect. Well, that's all right then. Poor old Orinoco—not like him to lose his appetite.'

'Can we see the rest of the burrow now, please?' asked Tomsk, licking his paws. He was a bit scared that if he didn't have some exercise he might not have much of an appetite for lunch.

'Certainly.' Dalai Gartok hit a small gong and a second later Cousin One appeared in the doorway and led the Wimbledon Wombles off on a conducted tour. Tomsk enjoyed every minute of it because it was his ideal burrow: there were climbing rooms, a gymnasium and a training department where a group of young Great White Wombles were being taught to leap. Tomsk enrolled at once in the training scheme, while Wellington was captivated by the Workshop, in which all kinds of mountaineering equipment was being taken to pieces, examined and then put to various uses. Behind the Workshop was an even more fascinating section of the burrow, full of enormous wheels.

'These wheels,' said Cousin One, 'are so delicately made that, with one small paw-push at the start of their lives, they can keep going round almost for ever. It is from these wheels that we get the power for our light globes, heating, water and cooking.'

'Oh, I do wish Tobermory could be here,' said Wellington, writing for all he was worth. 'He'd be ever so interested. It's all quite different from

95

Wimbledon, you know. Sorry, you were saying?'

So what with one thing and another it was hardly surprising that the time seemed to flash past, and it was with great regret that Tomsk and Wellington left the burrow of their Tibetan cousins the following day. They were warm, well-fed and they had slept for ten hours; and they were quite different from the two, scared, shivery Wombles of twenty-four hours ago.

'It's been jolly nice,' said Wellington.

'Mmmm,' agreed Tomsk.

'We have enjoyed your visit,' said Dalai Gartok. 'Here is a small gift for Young Bulgaria. One of my scroll paintings.'

They clasped paws, bowed and then, walking backwards, Wellington and Tomsk left the burrow, which they had christened between themselves 'The Hall of the Mountain Wombles'. With them were their gigantic cousins—Numbers One, Two, Three and Four. Cousin One was holding the trolley like a tidy-bag—all the controls had been defrosted—while Cousin Two was trailing the balloon behind him. Wellington and Tomsk were riding piggyback on Cousins Three and Four.

When they reached the edge of the slope it was still so early that the mountains were in darkness, although the first yellow light was showing on the highest peaks far above. Cousin One with six quick treads inflated the balloon while Cousin Two fixed it to the trolley.

'Now watch,' said the two Great White Wombles.

It was an astonishing scene for, as the sun came up, the blue and indigo shadows danced down the mountains like curtains being lifted, and in the blue haze they could see mile after mile of Tibet coming into view.

'It's smashing,' rumbled Tomsk.

'Mmmmmm,' agreed Wellington. 'It's—it's like being on top of the world.'

'We call this the roof of the world,' said Cousin One.

They stood in silence for a while, watching mountain after mountain lose its shadows and turn sparkling, blinding white. It was so beautiful that even Wellington couldn't find the right words to say about it.

'You must go now; please fix tidied-up oxygen masks,' said Cousin One in his deep rumbling voice.

'Yes,' Wellington agreed. 'Thank you all very much. We shall never forget the Everest Womble burrow. It's probably the most beautiful burrow ever on the roof of the world. And, I say, sorry, but . . . if you are worried about leaving paw tracks in the snow, I've thought of a way of getting rid of them quite easily. I hope you don't mind me mentioning it?'

'What is the way?' rumbled Cousin Two.

'It's quite simple, really. The last Great White Womble in the group wears a belt and attached to the belt is a kind of shawl, a bit like Dalai Gartok's, actually. And in the bottom of the shawl you have little wooden teeth, rather like a garden rake. So as the last Great White Womble walks over the snow he gets rid of all the pawmarks. I'm sure Tobermory would have thought of something better, but I do think this might work quite well. Oh dear!'

Wellington stopped talking and closed his eyes

97

tightly. It was very strange, but here he was almost at the top of Everest with just Tomsk and Cousins One, Two, Three and Four and yet in some mysterious way Dalai Gartok appeared to be standing right beside him.

'What a good idea,' said Dalai Gartok softly. 'Thank you so very much, Wellington.'

'Not at all. Pleasure,' mumbled Wellington and bowed.

Dalai Gartok bowed back and vanished.

'Finished?' said Tomsk. 'Time we were off, you know.'

'Sorry, yes,' said Wellington. 'We'd better go through the lift-off procedure.'

Everyone shook paws, then Tomsk and Wellington climbed into the trolley, the anchor was released and the balloon (which now looked gold-coloured in the sunshine) rose upwards. The four Cousins raised their paws. One moment they were there and the next they seemed to have vanished, as their long white fur became one with the sparkling snow.

'Very nice sort of Wombles,' rumbled Tomsk. 'I liked it there, didn't you, Wellington?'

'Mm,' agreed Wellington. 'Goodness, imagine us being related to the Great White Wombles of Tibet. I say, Tomsk, sorry, but you've got that reading wrong. We're heading due south now. Next stop Australia. Have a lichen pie.'

'Don't mind if I do,' said Tomsk as Balloon Two billowed gently over the top of Mount Everest.

CHAPTER 8½

CROSSED LINES

'I'll tell you what,' said Alderney to Shansi, 'I think I've got typist's cramp. Great Uncle Bulgaria goes on and on writing notes and I just can't keep up with him.'

'Alas,' agreed Shansi, rubbing her own fingers. 'I too am working all the time making out lists. Milk cartons to Cousin Botany. Pens to the Womblegarten, tin cans to the Workshop. It never stops.'

'I'll be glad when Wellington is back,' said Alderney. 'I never realised till now how much work he did . . .'

'Even Orinoco was quite busy, when not sleeping or eating,' said Shansi.

'And Tomsk was ever so good about carrying rubbish and shifting things and doing odd jobs around the burrow . . .'

The two young Wombles sighed and looked at

99

each other.

'Even Bungo wasn't too bad, really,' said Alderney, 'and it's so quiet with them all away. Nothing seems to happen except work . . .'

Now at that particular moment at least six different things happened at once. For a start the weather suddenly changed and the wind veered round from the north-east to the south-west; but Tobermory was so busy in the Workshop he didn't notice it. This was because the Womblegarten had been trying to show what very good working Wombles they could be, and so they had cleared up about twice as much rubbish as anybody else had ever done before. With the result, of course, that poor Tobermory didn't know whether he was on his back or his front paws, as the Workshop was practically overflowing with litter.

'Silly idea sending young Wellington off like that,' muttered Tobermory, 'when I need him here. Oh dear, oh me, I'll never get straight . . . Where's that Shansi then?'

And Tobermory, looking quite distracted, hurried past the barometer, giving it a tap as he went, but not bothering to notice that the needle had swung right across from left to right as he picked up his phone.

'*Tsk, tsk, tsk,*' said Great Uncle Bulgaria in his study, 'here I am with Chapter Nine nearly written, and a very interesting chapter it is too as it concerns the rebuilding of Tibbet's Corner and our long trek to Hyde Park, and there's nobody to copy out my notes. Bungo was quite good at that sort of thing. Silly sort of name, but he's really not too bad. Now where is Alderney . . . ?' And Great Uncle Bulgaria reached for his inter-burrow-phone.

'*Tiens*,' said Madame Cholet, stirring away at a delicious-smelling stew, 'does this taste right or does it not? Umm, yes, I think so. Maybe a touch more of dandelion salt. How dear little Orinoco would enjoy this stew. *Pauvre* Orinoco, where is he now, I ask myself? Probably starving to death in the middle of nowhere. No, never. He will always find food, that one. Oh, all this washing-up and I have no help as Alderney is doing her typewriting. Well, it is too bad. She will have to come and aid me for the moment . . .'

Madame Cholet put down her wooden spoon and took the kitchen phone off the hook.

'Dear me, dear, dear me,' said Miss Adelaide in the Womblegarten, 'there are all these exercise books to be corrected and the sums to be set for tomorrow morning. Added to which I have to work out the rota for tidying-up on the Common. It is all too much to be asked of one Womble. I simply must have help. Shansi must be released from her duties in the Workshop and returned to me. *Tsk, tsk, tsk.*'

Miss Adelaide picked up her inter-burrow-phone with her silky-grey paw.

The fifth thing that happened was that all these four calls went through to the burrow exchange at almost exactly the same moment. The very small Womble operator on duty had, with great care up until now, just about managed to deal with one call at a time every five minutes. But when four lights lit up within seconds of each other, her fingers became all thumbs and she got into a panic, and in no time at all she had got the lines crossed, so that Great Uncle Bulgaria found himself getting very

101

tetchy with Miss Adelaide—before he recognised whom he was talking to. When he did realise who it was, he got a great deal less tetchy, but by then it was too late. Meanwhile Madame Cholet, Tobermory, Alderney and Shansi were all on crossed lines and all talking at once.

The sixth thing, and really the most important, was that the ice on Queen's Mere started to crack and go soft just as a little Womble was in the middle of it, trying to tidy up a plastic bag. The ice made a soft, shivering sound and then gave way with a loud cracking noise.

'*Woow*, help,' shouted the little Womble, as his back paws sank into the icy water.

Fortunately for him, Cousin Botany was walking past at the time and heard this desperate cry.

'Now what?' said Cousin Botany, peering over the top of his spectacles, 'there's no peace these days, no tranquillity. Oh, my word! Hold still, young Womble, and don't move. Cousin Botany's coming.'

And, with a surprising burst of speed, Cousin Botany put down his gardening basket and trowel and skidded down the bank. He still had his gardening rake in one grey paw, and he lay down on his stomach on the ice and held the rake out at arm's length.

'Grab a hold of that then,' said Botany in his slow drawl.

The small Womble tried to do as he was told, but his fingers had gone all cold and stiff, so that the rake just slid away and at the same moment the ice cracked even more.

'*Yow*,' squeaked the small Womble and down into the icy water he went, vanishing completely except for the trailing edge of his scarf which had got hooked on a sharp piece of broken ice.

Fortunately for him, Cousin Botany was not the sort of Womble to panic. He just edged forward a little more and muttered slowly under his breath, 'One, two for him to go down, three for him to touch the bottom, four and five for him to bob up again . . . here he comes . . . gotcha!'

Cousin Botany was perfectly right, as at that precise second up bobbed the small Womble with his fur all stiff from fright and cold. Cousin Botany had got the teeth of the rake through the scarf and he gave a tremendous pull, and the small Womble found himself being hauled slithering and squawling across the ice, first on his front, then on his back and finally head over heels until he landed with a thump behind Cousin Botany.

'Silly little Womble,' said Cousin Botany,

103

groaning a bit as he got to his feet, and he undid the scarf and picked up the little Womble by his back paws and shook him violently. This was not because he was in a temper, but because he wanted his small relation to get rid of any water in his lungs. The little Womble was obligingly very sick and then burst into tears of fright and relief.

'Stop that,' ordered Cousin Botany. 'You're perfectly safe now,' and he tucked the small Womble under his arm and marched off back to the burrow, with the rake over his free shoulder.

The small Womble stopped shivering and sobbing when he found himself plumped down in the middle of the nice, warm kitchen, with Madame Cholet going '*tiens*' nineteen to the dozen while she wrapped a cosy blanket round him and poured piping hot acorn juice into a mug.

'And 'ow 'as this 'appened?' demanded Madame Cholet.

'No good getting in a tizzy with me, Madame. I'm going to have a word with that Tobermory. He's the one that's supposed to put up a notice when a thaw sets in!'

And off stumped Cousin Botany before Madame Cholet could get in another word, which was unfortunate as she would have liked to have explained that Tobermory was not in the best of tempers at the moment.

Cousin Botany soon discovered this, for he only got as far as '. . . and what's more, Tobermory, it'd have been your fault for not posting a Thaw Notice if that little jackaroo had been drowned . . .'

Tobermory threw down his clipboard and shouted, 'Thaw Notice! Thaw Notice! When have I got the time to do that, eh? Look at this

Workshop, just look at it! I'm up to my ears in rubbish and what's more I've got no help with it. That young Shansi's gone off somewhere skylarking about and . . .'

'Shansi,' said Miss Adelaide from the doorway, 'is helping me, Tobermory. I too have my problems! The new term's work schedule is lagging behind badly, there's the Womblegarten's tidying-up rota for tomorrow to be prepared AND I am the one who has to escort them round the Common . . .'

'Pity you didn't keep an eye on the one that nearly drowned . . .' Cousin Botany said unwisely.

'I CANNOT BE EVERYWHERE AT ONCE!'

'What's all this noise?' demanded Great Uncle Bulgaria. 'Really, I can't hear myself think, let alone write, in my study. And *where* is Alderney?'

'She is assisting me, Monsieur Bulgaria!' replied Madame Cholet, who had also come to see what the fuss was about. She was carrying a rolling pin in one hand and a dripping, dirty scarf in the other, and was looking unusually fierce for her.

'It's not my fault,' put in Alderney from behind Madame Cholet. 'I can't do all that typewriting and the washing-up as well . . .'

Shansi, who was clinging on to Alderney, tried to explain her position too, but her soft little voice was lost as everybody began to talk at once, and very loudly.

The small Womble, who had really sparked off all the trouble, shuffled into the doorway, his cheeks bulging with hot moss buns and the blanket trailing behind him. He'd had a terrible fright and he was scared by all the cross voices. Suddenly his face puckered and he went, *'Ooooooooow!'* at the top of his voice.

A great many of the Womblegarten, most of whom were tired out from doing so much tidying-up work, and who were standing out in the passage, all began to pucker up their faces too, and a general '*oooooow!*' broke out.

It was a wailing sound that was seldom if ever heard in the Wimbledon Burrow, and it stopped all the older Wombles in their tracks.

'THAT'S ENOUGH!' said Great Uncle Bulgaria. 'Be quiet, please.'

The howling died down into a 'sniff-sniff-hiccup'.

Great Uncle Bulgaria moved forward a little and leant heavily on his stick. Then he hitched up his shawl and looked over the top of his spectacles at everyone. He did it very slowly and thoughtfully, and even Miss Adelaide went quiet and stopped sniffing at the back of her nose.

'The trouble is,' said Great Uncle Bulgaria, 'that we've all been trying to do far too much. Tobermory is overwhelmed with the rubbish which the Womblegarten have worked so very hard to collect. Miss Adelaide has what I believe is now called too much workload. An ugly expression, but descriptive. Madame Cholet appears to be cooking and washing up night and day, because Alderney has been helping me. And Shansi has been trying to do two jobs at once. So we've all got overtired and cross and upset and unlike ourselves. Hm?'

There was a general hum of assent.

'Exactly. What is more, it's all my fault!'

'Never,' said Tobermory.

'Now, now, Great Uncle Bulgaria,' murmured Miss Adelaide.

Madame Cholet put the rolling pin under her

arm and shrugged so that her shoulders came right up to the top of her ears.

'Too right,' said Cousin Botany slowly.

'Too right, indeed. Another expressive phrase. Therefore, I have decided that we must do something about the situation. Something very drastic indeed.'

Great Uncle Bulgaria paused and everybody held their breath. The old Womble's little round eyes twinkled as he looked at their anxious faces.

'What we're going to do,' he said gently, 'is to stop being silly and cross and bad-tempered and tired. We're going to have a holiday from work. I shall stop writing, Tobermory will let the rubbish stay where it is, Miss Adelaide will forget all about rotas and correcting lessons and Madame Cholet can stop cooking.'

There was an absolute buzz of astonishment which was stilled by Madame Cholet saying, 'Monsieur Bulgaria, that is all very well, but if I do not cook what shall we eat?'

Great Uncle Bulgaria leant forward and tapped the barometer with his stick, at which the needle moved right round to 'Fair and Warm'.

'Spring is really here now. There will be nettles and moss, clover and daisies and buttercups on the Common . . .'

'Too right and plenty of good waterweed as well,' said Cousin Botany. 'I noticed it this afternoon when the ice broke. I had meant to mention it before, but it slipped me mind. What with one thing and another . . .'

'So we'll have a two-day picnic,' went on Great Uncle Bulgaria, giving Cousin Botany the ghost of a wink. 'Do us all good and I dare say the

107

Womblegarten might like to have some kind of sports day, hm, Miss Adelaide?'

'It might be a good idea,' said Miss Adelaide, by which she meant that it was a very good idea indeed. 'However, it will take a lot of planning.'

'Yes, indeed. Let *them* plan it. Here, you in the blanket with your mouth open, why don't you plan it, hm? An acorn and spoon race? Jumping the bushes hurdles? A long jump? Think you could manage it?'

The small Womble shut his mouth with a snap and nodded violently. Then he turned round and pushed the rest of the Womblegarten ahead of him, whispering and shoving until the last of them disappeared in the direction of the Playroom.

'Got another young Bungo there, I shouldn't be surprised,' said Tobermory in a dry voice. 'Well, all right then, Bulgaria. I'm on.'

'I suppose they'll manage,' said Miss Adelaide a shade doubtfully.

'Make an awful job of it probably,' said Cousin Botany, 'but do 'em a power of good. Well, I'm off to take a look at that waterweed. Very nice it was. Might take a cutting or two for my greenhouses and see how . . .'

Cousin Botany nodded a couple of times and left, still muttering under his breath as he went.

'No cooking,' said Madame Cholet, sinking down on a packing case which had . . . YFFES BANANA stencilled on it. '*Tiens*. I very much enjoy making meals, you understand, but it will be very pleasant to have *le holiday* . . .'

'I love picnics,' said Alderney, 'and, just think, no typewriting or washing-up for two whole days! Smashing!'

'No lists, no rotas, no rushing, no crossness,' murmured Shansi.

'Exactly,' agreed Great Uncle Bulgaria. He sniffed suddenly and then said, 'Excuse me, Madame Cholet, but—er—is everything all right in the kitchen?'

'My elmbark casserole!' exclaimed Madame Cholet, springing to her feet. 'I put it in the oven hours ago. Tonight we all have a hot meal, but tomorrow, Monsieur Bulgaria, it is *le picnic. Oui?*'

'*Oui*,' agreed Great Uncle Bulgaria.

CHAPTER 9

CHINATOWN

'Cor, it's hot,' said Orinoco.

'Never known it so warm for the time of year,' agreed Cousin Yellowstone, using his broad-brimmed hat like a fan.

Bungo was, unusually for him, beyond speech.

Only Idaho, sitting cross-legged and cross-armed in the shade of an immensely tall redwood tree seemed undistressed by the heat.

'Why don't we go down to the coast?' he suggested. 'Bound to be a bit of a breeze off the sea there.'

'Good thinking,' said Cousin Yellowstone. 'Well, have you seen enough of the forest?'

'Never seen anything like it before in my life,' said Orinoco truthfully as he looked up and up and up at the great trees, which seemed to go on for ever. A fat ground squirrel, with its short tail, came hopping across the grass and nibbled at a nut

110

which it held delicately between its front paws.

'They're quite different—but just as silly—as the Wimbledon Common squirrels. Don't they *ever* climb trees?' asked Orinoco.

'Never, not built for it,' said Cousin Yellowstone. 'Hi there, young Bungo, wake up now. What do you think of this neck of the woods? Hm?'

Bungo blinked, stretched and sat up sleepily.

'It's those hotel—no, motel—places that I liked,' he said. 'American Human Beings seem to like living out of doors, don't they? That swimming pool in the last motel place was smashing. Tomsk would've liked it. I did. Actually it's the only time I've felt cool.'

'You swim real good,' agreed Idaho, who had watched Bungo practising his Womble crawl up and down the pool at sunrise.

'What I can't get over,' said Orinoco, waking up completely, 'is all that food your Human Beings put out in plastic bags. Lots and lots of perfectly good food. Your American Wombles can't ever be hungry.'

'Agreed,' said Cousin Yellowstone. 'Our deep freezes are rarely empty. Our big problem is the objects we tidy up, most of which are some sort of plastic. Plastic is not an easy kind of material to make good use of.'

'Tobermory often says that,' said Orinoco. 'What he says is . . .'

'Problems, problems,' said Cousin Yellowstone, starting to laugh. 'Good old Tobermory, I can just hear him doing it. OK, let's go.'

'Where to?' asked Bungo, tidily sweeping up his iced clover lolly-stick.

'The coast,' said Idaho. 'The western seaboard. You've seen just about everything else. The Middle West, the Grand Canyon, the old Wild West towns, the gold diggings, the East Coast, the Prairies, the Deep South . . .'

'Um, lovely food there was there,' said Orinoco with a happy smile. 'Some of the very best food I've ever eaten actually. I'll tell you what I remember about *that*. Chocolate-covered acorn pancakes with whipped daisy cream, waffles with clover syrup, nutties loaded with cream, blueberry pudding, bracken batter cakes, cream of wheat, Womble special three-deckers, nut . . .'

'You've got jolly fat,' said Bungo, pulling his friend up on to his feet, as Orinoco, with an enormous smile on his face, leafed through all the notes which he had so thoughtfully taken for Madame Cholet.

'I'm just exactly the right size for a Womble,' replied Orinoco in a dignified manner.

'If you get much fatter Balloon One won't get up into the air at all!'

'Shut up.'

'Shut up yourself.'

Orinoco cuffed Bungo and Bungo hit him back, at which Idaho forgot to be quiet and dignified and took a flying dive at both of them, and a most enjoyable fight was had by all three.

'OK, OK, OK,' said Cousin Yellowstone, marching into the middle of the fray and ending it by the simple means of tucking two struggling Wombles under one arm and picking up the third by the scruff of his neck and shaking him.

'It's too hot to tangle. Darn it, don't know what's got into the weather. C'mon, we're going to the coast to cool down.'

The three young Wombles, now in the best of tempers as there is nothing like a good scuffle between friends to make a Womble stop feeling scratchy, hot and irritable, found themselves dumped in the back of the clockwork pickup.

'How about a song?' suggested Idaho as the warm wind blew through their fur. 'One, two, three. *Go down, Wombles, go down . . .*'

'*Go down,*' sang Orinoco in a deep voice.

'*Go down . . .*' warbled Bungo.

'*Go down, Wombles,*' they chorused together. '*Go down . . .*'

'*Go down and pick up all that trash-can-litter-rubbish-and-*ALL,' roared Cousin Yellowstone. 'Go down, Wombles . . .'

They sang and thumped their back paws all the way through the great forest, much to the astonishment of the ground squirrels and the deer who, with huge almond-shaped eyes, looked even more surprised than usual. However, as they were quite used to Womble litter-details in the forest, they weren't in the least frightened. In fact, in their own shy way, they were glad to see them, as many a young fawn had been stopped from choking to death on a plastic bag, or been freed from a jagged tin, by a helpful, if bossy, member of the Womble clear-up group.

'We'll make camp tonight,' said Cousin Yellowstone, as they reached the end of the forest, 'so that we can get to the coast early morning. OK?'

'OK,' chorused the three young Wombles, who had by now started to doze off again.

Cousin Yellowstone, who was thoroughly

113

enjoying getting away from the responsibilities of running his burrow, gathered together a lot of fallen wood and whistled softly to himself as he worked. It really made him feel quite young again to be living out under the stars, and he sighed a little as he remembered the old days when he had worked his way from east to west living from paw to mouth. Idaho was happy too as he got the cooking-pot going and Orinoco was only too pleased to assist him.

'Waffles?' he asked, his eyes gleaming in the starlight.

'Waffles coming up,' replied Idaho.

'Smashing,' said Bungo, who had been trotting about looking important, but who hadn't, in fact, been doing very much. 'I'll tell you what, it's jolly nice being a Womble in America. It's . . . it's so big, you know.'

'Correct,' agreed Cousin Yellowstone. 'Well, the burrow's made. How about some food, hm?'

It was before dawn when they left the great forest. Not even the earliest of the early birds were stirring as they made for the coast, and the slight breeze was refreshingly cool on their faces as they travelled westwards. They reached San Francisco just in time to see the sun come up, and for just a moment the famous bridge did look as if it were made of gold.

'Fisherman's Wharf,' said Cousin Yellowstone. 'Put on your coveralls and caps.'

Bungo and Orinoco obediently slid into what they would have called overalls, and looked at what lay before them.

'Goodness,' said Bungo, 'doesn't this place go up and down a lot?'

'Even more than Wimbledon High Street,' agreed Orinoco. 'I say, what a very nice smell.'

'That is the sea,' said Idaho coldly.

'No, it isn't, it's food,' replied Orinoco. 'Well, of course, it could be the sea as well, I dare say.'

Cousin Yellowstone parked the truck and the four Wombles ambled up and down the quayside, looking round-eyed at the stalls, which were absolutely covered in all kinds of marine life like crabs, clams, shellfish, lobsters, sand dabs and soles.

'I can't like it,' said Bungo in a small voice. 'I know it's all very interesting and that, but I honestly can't like it. Can you, Orinoco?'

'No. It's all right for Human Beings, I suppose, but not for Wombles. Oh . . . look!'

Orinoco pointed with a small fat paw and Bungo was just in time to see some sleek pelicans flapping across the sky. As pelicans are extremely rare on Wimbledon Common, the two young Wombles were very interested. What was even more rare, so rare indeed that neither of them had ever seen it before, was a smooth face suddenly rising out of the sea. It had round black eyes and a moustache and it opened its mouth and went *'Aaaark!'*

'It's Nessie!' exclaimed Bungo, grabbing at Orinoco. 'It's Cousin Nessie, the Water-Womble from Loch Ness.'

' 'Course it isn't,' said Orinoco. 'Nessie hasn't got a moustache. Mind you, it is a bit like a Tobermory Water-Womble . . . no, it's a—a—um sea lion. And *aaaaaark* to you.'

The sea lion barked back, put up its flipper, did a backwards somersault and vanished into the Pacific.

115

'Seen enough?' asked Cousin Yellowstone. 'Well, while it's still cool, we'd better have a trip on the trolleys. This way.'

A 'trip on the trolleys' turned out to be an absolutely fascinating and rather fur-raising journey on a cable car which, like the pelicans, went swooping up and down over the hills of San Francisco. As, even at that early hour, the cable cars were full, Bungo, Orinoco and Idaho found that they had to cling to the outside of the car. It was very exciting, especially when they reached a crossroads, as the cable car driver didn't bother to slow down, but just went *ding ding ding* very loudly on his bell, expecting all other traffic to get out of his way. Luckily it always did so.

Cousin Yellowstone wisely stayed inside the cable car, where he had found himself a nice, comfortable seat near the driver. The two of them struck up a conversation which they both thoroughly enjoyed, as it was all about what they called The Good Old Days when, according to them, Everything Was Much Better.

'Don't know when I've had a nicer talk,' said the driver at the end of the trip, 'Glad to know you, sir.'

'Glad to know *you*,' said Cousin Yellowstone. 'Thank you kindly.'

Cousin Yellowstone bowed politely and climbed down and went and unstuck Idaho, Bungo and Orinoco who, being Wombles, were still clinging tenaciously to the outside of the cable car.

'Last port of call, Chinatown,' said Cousin Yellowstone. 'Back to the truck.'

'*China*town?' Bungo whispered to Orinoco behind his paw, wishing for the first time in his young life that he had paid more attention to Miss Adelaide's Geography lessons. 'I say, I thought a Chinese sort of town would be in China, you know, and this is America.'

' 'Course this is America. But you can have Chinese towns all over the place. Dare say there's one in Wimbledon somewhere,' replied Orinoco, who was pretty hazy about this situation himself. But being older than Bungo he wasn't, naturally enough, going to admit to this.

'Chinatown,' announced Cousin Yellowstone in his deep voice. 'Everybody out now, and mind, keep together.'

It was just like stepping into another country. Instead of the skyscrapers which had quite taken their breath away in New York, or the dignified and enormous buildings of Washington, or even the elegant houses of New Orleans, the Wimbledon Wombles saw before them a criss-cross of narrow streets and small buildings which were absolutely packed with stalls, fluttering signs and Human Beings. What is more there was rubbish everywhere.

'I felt you should see this,' said Cousin Yellowstone in a mournful voice, 'so that you would realise that we have a great many problems in some parts of the States. This is one of them.'

'Cor,' agreed Bungo.

'But it smells nice,' said Orinoco, sniffing deeply. 'I expect they are good cooks, these Chinese Town Human Beings.'

'That's as may be but, like most Human Beings, they don't clear up very well,' said Cousin Yellowstone heavily.

Keeping very close together, the four Wombles

walked up and down the narrow streets until Orinoco could bear all the delicious smells no longer.

'Mushroom chop suey, if I'm not mistaken,' he said. 'Cousin Yellowstone, I'm starving. Can I make a few notes please? Just for Madame Cholet, you know.'

'OK,' said Cousin Yellowstone, 'but be careful.'

'Trust me,' said Orinoco and disappeared round the back of the restaurant from which all these lovely smells were issuing. His sharp little nose took him instantly to a particularly large black plastic bag, and he was just about to put in a paw when a soft voice said, 'Can help, please?' Orinoco stopped dead and then very slowly turned round, to find himself face to face with a small figure who was bowing and nodding.

'It all depends,' said Orinoco cautiously, 'what you mean by help, you know. What's your name?'

'Nanking is my name. Nanking Womble.'

'Never!' said Orinoco. 'I'm pleased to meet you. Orinoco, Orinoco Womble. Shake a paw. I say, did I get a sniff of mushroom chop suey just now? I'm starving. Very hungry, that is. So are my friends. Would there be any to spare?'

'Always plenty spare,' said Nanking, bowing and nodding harder than ever. 'Please invite Womble friends to join us inside. Yes?'

'*Rather,*' said Orinoco.

It was over two hours later that four rather fat-looking Wombles emerged into the street, rubbing their stomachs and scratching behind their ears.

'Well, I must say,' murmured Cousin Yellowstone, 'I've learnt more about the problems of Chinatown during the last hundred and twenty

118

minutes or so than ever before. I'd no idea there was a Chinese Womble community right here under our noses, and what problems they have! Orinoco, thank you.'

' 'S all right,' said Orinoco who was busy scribbling down the cooking instructions which Nanking had given him. 'Good cooks, these Chinese Wombles. I wonder if we could grow bean shoots on Wimbledon Common? I'll have to ask Cousin Botany when we get home.'

'It'll be awfully nice to get back to Wimbledon Common,' said Bungo, quite forgetting that he was supposed to be a great explorer and brave adventurer.

'Sure it will,' said Cousin Yellowstone. 'I sometimes feel homesick for the old burrow myself. Never mind, young Womble, you only have one more country to visit, and then you can set sail—or balloon—for Wimbledon. Meanwhile, back to the truck . . .'

'One more country,' said Bungo, 'and do you know what country that is? I'll tell you what it is— it's Japan and it'll take ages and ages and AGES to get there.'

'No, it won't,' said Idaho as they walked back to the truck, and he licked one finger and stuck it up into the air. 'Wind has changed. Weather has changed. You will reach Japan very fast.'

'Oh, get on,' said Bungo, starting to smile. 'You don't know anything about the weather. You're just doing your Native American Womble act.'

'No, never,' said Idaho, crossing his arms and grunting.

'Yes, you are.'

'No, I'm not . . .'

'Oh, shut up,' interrupted Orinoco. 'How can I get down the last of Nanking's recipe if you keep on arguing? Now, was it four ounces of mushrooms or five? Or, hang on a moment, perhaps it was three . . . what are you two laughing about? I'll have you know that it's very important to get these things right, don't you agree, Cousin Yellowstone?'

'I do indeed,' said Cousin Yellowstone 'and what's more, it's also important for me to get you two Wimbledon Wombles back to your transport. Lift-off time is just three hours away, according to Tobermory's schedule!'

CHAPTER 10

GREAT-GREAT AUNT M. MURRUMBIDGEE

Tomsk was singing, somewhat off-key, a tune that he couldn't get out of his head. Then he stopped singing and said, 'Who *is* Waltzing Matilda, Wellington?'

'Sorry, don't know,' replied Wellington who was writing up his notes. As he had made himself a hat out of paper, and was wearing it over his cap, he looked rather odd; but Tomsk's appearance was even stranger, as he was wearing a kind of paper bonnet.

'My word, it's warm,' muttered Tomsk, flapping a cardboard fan.

The two young Wombles glanced up at the sky which was a dazzling blue dotted with fluffy little white clouds.

'Wouldn't suit our big Cousins,' said Wellington, snapping his notebook shut and yawning. 'I wonder what the Australian ones will be like?

121

Well, we'll soon find out—it shouldn't be too long now. Goodness, we seem to have been flying over this country for days and days.'

'*And* days. Empty sort of place, isn't it?'

They got to their back paws and looked over the edge of the trolley. Below them was mile after mile of brownish grass, with here and there a clump of tall bushes, and now and again a long straight road whose beginning and end vanished in the heat haze. Every so often a small figure would go bounding from one group of bushes to the next.

'Bit like the Tibetan Wombles,' said Tomsk.

'They're kangaroos. I remember Cousin Botany telling me once about when he was young and gave an injured kangaroo his hat to wear. He said he never did get his hat back. Perhaps it's still jumping about down there!'

'Be pretty old by now, I should think. I say, Wellington, look at that car down there. Funny sort of shape.'

Wellington followed the direction in which Tomsk was pointing and stared. The car, if car it was, wasn't travelling on a road, but was going quite fast over open country. Even from this height, they could see that it had what appeared to be a park bench as the back seat, with an old-fashioned bedrail behind it. Two small figures wearing large hats were sitting in the front, and they looked as if they were peering through a windscreen made of proper windows.

'It's . . . it's stopping,' said Wellington nervously. 'I wonder if they've spotted us? What's more it's stopped just where we're supposed to land. Oh dear. Now what do we do?'

'Better do what Tobermory ordered,' replied

122

Tomsk firmly. Even though he was thousands of miles from Wimbledon, he didn't want to go against Tobermory's instructions.

'Tobermory's never wrong,' Tomsk added vaguely, 'and if those Human Beings do start being nosy we can always take off again.'

'Um. Yes. I say, look!'

They looked. Not only had the car stopped at exactly the point where their balloon was supposed to land, but the driver had climbed out and was turning a handle at the side of the steering wheel. A kind of aerial with a flag attached to the top of it appeared. The aerial grew taller until it was about six feet high and then stopped. The flag fluttered gently in a faint breeze.

'Got a "W" on it,' reported Tomsk, who has astonishingly good eyesight—even for a Womble. 'Wonder what that stands for?'

But Wellington was too busy going through the landing procedure to listen to what Tomsk was saying. They might be nosy Human Beings down there, but the lazy flapping of the flag was certainly a great help in working out the wind speed, with the result that Balloon Two made—for the first time—an absolutely perfect landing in exactly the right spot.

'Off Props,' said Wellington.

'Off Props,' rumbled Tomsk.

'Well, here they come,' said Wellington, his paw on the Emergency Take-Off control—just in case there was trouble.

Two small figures, their faces shadowed by their large hats, came trotting across the brown scrub.

'Hallo,' said the first stranger and stuck out a paw. 'Welcome to Australia. You'll be Wellington?

I'm Cairns. This is Perth.'

'Hallo,' said Perth, 'and you'll be Tomsk. Welcome to Australia. Good trip?'

'You're . . . you're Wombles!' said Wellington.

'Too right we are. What did you think we were, Human Beings?'

'Well, sorry, yes, just for a minute we did wonder. I say, how do you do!' said Wellington. 'Goodness, it's jolly nice to be here. And thank you for putting up that flag thing—it was a great help.'

Everybody then shook paws with everybody else several times over, until Cairns said, 'Well, better stack that flying machine of yours away in the back of the old car here. Can't keep the burrow waiting.'

'It's a very unusual sort of car, isn't it?' said Wellington, once the balloon had been deflated and stacked neatly inside the trolley, which in turn was roped to the back of what he could now see was definitely a garden seat.

'That's right,' agreed Cairns. 'Our very own design. Made up of all kinds of throw-outs. Park bench in the back, easy chairs in the front. Steering wheel comes from a boat, indicators from an old ute.'

'Ute?'

'Utility truck. So we call this car our Ute-Beaut. Goes anywhere, no trouble at all, and runs on clockwork. Hold on while I wind her up.'

It was a surprisingly smooth journey across country, for the Ute-Beaut had balloon-like tyres which cushioned them against bumps.

''Course we don't use her in the cities,' said Cairns, who was driving, 'but she's great out here in the country.'

'Isn't this the—er—Outback?' asked

124

Wellington, who had been looking at his maps.

'Nah, the Outback's over there,' replied Perth, waving a paw towards the hazy horizon. 'The Outback's always miles and miles away, wherever you are. Human Beings and even Wombles don't ever say they're in it.'

'Sorry, but why not?'

'Too big. Makes you feel sort of lost. Look, camels . . .'

'I didn't know there were camels here!'

'You do now.'

'Too right,' Wellington heard himself saying. 'I mean, goodness, yes. We saw some kangaroos as well.'

'Roos we call 'em. Silly sort of animal, but quite friendly. Don't talk much, though. Here we are— home.'

Home appeared to be nothing but a large bank surrounded by thorn trees, but as the Ute-Beaut reached it, the sparse vegetation stirred and a drawbridge came down. Cairns drove straight over it and into the burrow, coming to a halt in a cloud of dust.

'Hallo, hallo, hallo,' said a voice and a small, grey-brown Womble appeared out of the haze. She was wearing a large hat, a sleeveless coat and an apron, and she looked extremely fierce.

'So, you took your time,' she said. 'I'm your Great-great Aunt M. Murrumbidgee. Hallo.'

The small Womble held out a paw, and Wellington and Tomsk shook it without a word to say for themselves.

'Cat got your tongues?' said Great-great Aunt M. Murrumbidgee. 'Didn't expect to see me here, I dare say. Although Botany should have told you.

Come on in and have a thorn-bush juice. There's nothing goes on in Australia that's to do with Wombles that I don't know about. Well, sit down, sit down. Poor-looking pair you are. It's all that city life you lead right in the middle of London, I dare say. What you need is good fresh air and exercise.'

'Wimbledon isn't in the middle . . .' Wellington said feebly.

' 'Tis to me. No room to breathe there and don't argue. I know what's best. Cairns, Perth, stable that Ute-Beaut of yours. And quick.'

'Yes, OK, Great-great Aunt . . .'

The Ute Beaut clicked away and disappeared into the depths of the burrow and Great-great Aunt M. Murrumbidgee went *tsk, tsk, tsk* and hurried over to a speaking tube, took what looked like a wooden peg out of it and blew. There was a shrieking whistle that made the fur of Wellington and Tomsk stand up on end for a moment.

'Three thorn-bush specials and make sure they're iced, and a plate of bluegum waffles. Don't argue, do it. And quick. Well?'

This last 'well' was directed at Wellington who stared back dumbly.

'Aren't you going to take your hats off?' asked Great-great Aunt M. Murrumbidgee. 'In my young days it wasn't considered polite or good manners to sit around a burrow wearing hats. Maybe it's different in London. Hm?'

Wellington took off both his hats like a Womble in a trance, but Tomsk, after slowly removing his paper bonnet and thinking things over in his own time, said, 'Don't usually wear a hat. Sorry, I forgot it. But Wimbledon isn't in London. Wimbledon's a very nice place. The grass there is green, the air is nice and fresh and we take lots and lots of exercise. We do swimming and running and sports and golf and sometimes cricket. Think you've got it muddled up with somewhere else.'

Wellington shut his eyes and waited for the roof to fall in. He was quite certain that no other Womble had ever spoken like this before to Great-great Aunt M. Murrumbidgee, who in a way resembled Great Uncle Bulgaria, Miss Adelaide, Tobermory and Madame Cholet all rolled into one.

There was a long silence, during which Tomsk stared placidly at his Australian relative. Tomsk knew that he wasn't a clever sort of Womble like Wellington, but he did know when he was right about things. And one of the things about which he was absolutely certain was every kind of sport.

'Good on you,' said Great-great Aunt M. Murrumbidgee suddenly. 'I like a Womble who

127

knows his own mind. What kind of cricket do you play?'

'The usual sort. Eleven-a-side. I'm a pace bowler . . .'

'I might have known it! Hallo, here are our thorn-bush specials and the bluegum waffles. Put 'em down here. Tomsk, Wellington, I'd like you to meet Eucula, our cook-in-chief. And a very good cook she is too.'

Eucula wore a white, starched apron and had steel-rimmed spectacles halfway down her nose. Her fur was grey-grey-brown and her eyes over the top of her glasses were almost as sharp as Great-Great Aunt M. Murrumbidgee's. She slapped down three cartons of juice and a large plate of bluegum waffles and sniffed.

'So you're from Wimbledon, England,' she said. 'Never had bluegum waffles before, I dare say?'

'No, sorry,' said Wellington, coming out of his trance-like state, 'but that's because we haven't got bluegum trees on Wimbledon Common, you know. Of course we've got lots of other trees and bushes and Madame Cholet makes . . .'

'Madame Cholet,' said Eucula, suddenly becoming a great deal less stiff and starchy. 'Oh, I've often wished I could meet her. Her bracken pie with daisy sauce, now that sounds a real treat. I don't suppose you'd happen to know how she makes it?'

'Um,' said Wellington, wishing desperately that Orinoco was there, 'well, yes, actually, I think I can just about remember . . .'

'Well, just eat and drink up while I get out my notebook. Of course, I'll have to use thorn-bush roots instead of bracken. Now then?' And Eucula

128

produced a pencil from behind her ear.

'Um, I say, these waffles are smashing,' said Wellington rather thickly. 'Well, first of all you need . . .'

Meanwhile Tomsk, equally thickly, was talk- ing about cricket to Great-great Aunt M. Murrumbidgee; and for once in his life, he realised that he had met another Womble who knew just as much about googlies, off-spinners, bouncers and Chinamen as he did. As he'd never had a chance to talk really seriously about cricket before, he enjoyed it a great deal. What was more he got so carried away—which was most unlike Tomsk who was usually a silent sort of Womble—that he contradicted his very elderly Australian relation several times.

Cairns and Perth, who had tiptoed in to have a quick snack, held their breath. Not one of the New South Wales Wombles had ever dared to contradict Great-great Aunt M. Murrumbidgee. With their ears back and their paws poised for instant flight, they waited for Tomsk to be demolished. Instead of which, Great-great Aunt M. Murrumbidgee actually smiled and said, 'Well, I dunno, for a London sort of Womble you talk a lot of good sense, young Tomsk. I don't mind telling you when I heard over the Womblex that you were coming, I thought it was a lot of nonsense. However, if you really want to know what's been happening to us Australian Wombles, I dare say I wouldn't mind telling you. Young Wellington, get out that notebook of yours and stop going on about pies and puddings. Are you ready?'

'Ready,' said Wellington. 'However, sorry, but

first of all I must finish telling Eucula about moss-cream you know.'

Wellington is a very tidy-minded Womble and, once he has started to do something, he can't bear not to finish it properly. As he was about halfway through giving Eucula this particular recipe he couldn't stand the thought of not completing it. His voice was quite mild, but firm, and in a dim sort of way it reminded Tomsk of Great Uncle Bulgaria.

Great-great Aunt M. Murrumbidgee, who hadn't been spoken to in that tone of voice for a long, long time, stiffened, snorted and blinked her eyes. Cairns and Perth began to tiptoe backwards towards the door, Eucula went very still and Tomsk, who suddenly felt extremely weary, yawned as quietly as he could behind one paw.

'Oh, my word,' said Great-great Aunt M. Murrumbidgee. 'Well, I'd never have thought, to look at the pair of you, that you'd got so much of the old Outback Womble spirit in you! No, I wouldn't. All right, all right, I'll have to tell you about The Good Old Days when all we had to do was to clear up a tucker-bag or two. *Tsk, tsk, tsk.* 'Night all.'

'Goodnight,' said Tomsk and Wellington, politely getting to their back paws, and quite unaware that either of them had behaved in the least unexpectedly.

'Tell you what,' said Tomsk to Cairns and Perth, who were still standing rigidly to attention, 'I'd like to try out that left arm spin that Great Aunt—er—that she was talking about. Perhaps we could have a go tomorrow, mm?'

'Mm,' said Cairns and Perth. 'Mm, rather.'

130

'Now then,' said Wellington to Eucula, who for some strange reason was sniffing and snorting and blowing her nose, 'for the rest of the ingredients you need . . . I say, sorry, but is anything the matter?'

'Nothing,' said Eucula. 'Oh my goodness, I never thought to see the day when a couple of young London Wombles would get on the soft side of Great-great Aunt M. Murrumbidgee. Go on then, you were saying?'

'Well, you take two cartons of moss and . . .'

CHAPTER 11

CRACKERS, BALLOONS AND KITES

'Now this,' said Orinoco, 'is more like it.'

'It's all right,' agreed Bungo doubtfully, 'but a bit steamy. Are you there, Orinoco?'

' 'Course I'm there,' replied Orinoco, having a good stretch. 'It's like a nice warm fog, isn't it?'

Bungo nodded. He was wearing a very large towel and a doleful expression as he sat on a stone slab surrounded by clouds and clouds of hot steam. Somewhere in the middle of all that steam was Orinoco, also draped in a large towel. But, although he could hear Orinoco's voice and the stretching sounds, Bungo would have been a great deal happier if he could have actually seen his friend.

'It's a bit foreign, isn't it?' said Bungo in a whisper.

' 'Course it's foreign. This is Japan. Very clean sort of Wombles, the Japanese kind. Need to be, I expect, with all that smog and fog and stuff. Can't be very good for them,' replied Orinoco. 'Dare say they have a lot of falling fur and hard paw. You all right, Bungo?'

'Not *very* all right,' said Bungo in an uncertain voice. He wouldn't have cared to admit it, not even to Orinoco, with whom he had now shared dozens of adventures, but he was quite desperately homesick. He would have done a month's tidying-up work with no holidays at this very moment, if only he could have heard Great Uncle Bulgaria's voice telling him that Bungo was a silly sort of name, but that it suited him. It would have been equally wonderful to hear Tobermory going '*tsk, tsk, tsk*; problems, problems . . .'

'Mm,' mumbled Bungo.

'Now look here,' said Orinoco, suddenly appearing out of the hot mist with his towel draped over his head, 'this is the last country we're going to visit. And it's a very important country too. Can't quite remember why, but I know it is. Something to do with pollution and rubbish and that. Anyway, we're here and we've jolly well got to behave properly, so stop sniffing and blow your nose . . .'

'Haven't got a handkerchief . . .'

'You've got a perfectly good towel—use that. Just remember to keep bowing—they seem to like that, can't think why—and anyway the food'll be good. That's always something to look forward to.'

'Mmmm,' said Bungo, blowing his nose frantically on the edge of his towel.

'Nothing like food for making you feel cheerful,' said Orinoco, 'Hallo, something's happening. Thank goodness for that. All this washing and cleaning is very tiring. I haven't had a really good forty winks for days.'

The hot, steamy mist cleared slightly as a shutter was raised and a tiny Womble wearing a long and very pretty robe appeared. She bowed three times and said in a soft voice, 'Please to come this way. Yes?'

Orinoco bowed in return and gave Bungo a kick on the ankle. Bungo bowed and sniffed.

The tiny Womble shuffled forward at a surprising rate on her wooden sandals, and bowed again as she ushered them into a small changing room, where two beautifully embroidered dressing gowns were laid out. Beside them were Orinoco's broad-brimmed hat and Bungo's cap, and two pairs of wooden sandals.

What with the dressing gowns being rather long and the sandals rather difficult to walk in, the two Wimbledon Wombles soon discovered that the easiest way was to shuffle.

'In here, please,' said the tiny Womble, bowing again.

A bell sounded softly and Orinoco and Bungo, shuffling and tripping, found themselves in a medium-sized room. There were coloured pictures on the walls, two long, low tables and at the far end, a kind of small platform, on which sat a silky-grey Womble wearing a very splendid dressing gown indeed. He had what appeared to be two big knitting-needles criss-crossed at the back of his head, as a sort of decoration. He also had a long, drooping grey moustache and a small black silk cap tipped towards his nose.

Orinoco and Bungo considered themselves to be pretty widely travelled Wombles of the world by this time, but this personage was unlike any other Womble they had ever seen. They glanced at each other and then bowed deeply.

'Welcome,' said the grey Womble, bowing even more deeply. 'Welcome to our most humble burrow.'

'It's not at all humble—I think it looks like a jolly nice burrow,' said Orinoco politely. 'I'm Orinoco and this is Bungo.'

'Am Cousin Tokyo.'

'Honourable Cousin Tokyo,' said Orinoco, who had been doing his homework.

Honourable Cousin Tokyo took his front paws out of his sleeves and held them wide, as he went on in his soft voice, 'Please to sit down and eat.'

'Thanks,' said Orinoco. 'I *am* a bit peckish as it so happens. It's all this travelling about, I expect. It smells jolly nice, whatever it is.'

'So glad.'

However, even Orinoco's face fell a bit when an enormous and quite delicious-smelling dish was put in front of him, together with two small wooden sticks. He looked hopefully for a spoon or a fork, and then watched as Honourable Cousin Tokyo picked up his two sticks in one paw and dipped the ends into his bowl.

'Shouldn't be too difficult,' muttered Orinoco and, hoisting up the sleeve of his dressing gown, he tried to copy Honourable Cousin Tokyo. Being quite a quick learner when he put his mind to it, Orinoco was soon eating very fast indeed. He only got the food to his mouth about one time in every three, but, as the food, although unusual, was extremely tasty, he made up for what he missed by sheer speed.

Bungo, who was still suffering from bad home-sickness, didn't care too much and ate what he could off one stick.

'Amazing, astonishing,' said Honourable Cousin Tokyo as he looked at Orinoco. 'You will have some more, please?'

'Yes please, rather,' said Orinoco. 'Nice kind of food you have here. Tasty. Reminds me of the food we had in Chinatown.'

'You have been to China?'

'Not exactly,' said Orinoco through rather a large mouthful. 'Chinatown, you know, it's a place in America. Met some Chinese-American Wombles there. Got a lot of tidying-up problems.'

'Ah,' Honourable Cousin Tokyo sighed and nodded. 'We too have many such problems. Japanese Human Beings are thrifty and do not throw away much, but they have so many factories, cars and lorries. Much pollution in main cities. Japanese people making poison for themselves all the time. Many Human Beings have to wear mask.'

'Same thing in San Francisco,' agreed Orinoco. 'I say, could I have just one more tiny helping?'

'Help self.'

'Ta. How do you deal with it? Here, young Bungo, if you've finished eating you'd better make a few notes, you know. Great Uncle Bulgaria won't be at all pleased if you get home with empty pages in your book.'

'Empty pages in *my* book!' said Bungo, forgetting to be homesick because he was so indignant. 'There're hardly *any* full pages in your book.'

'Nonsense. Full of recipes and that. Get a move on and don't argue. Sorry, Honourable Cousin

Tokyo, you were saying?'

Bungo heaved an enormous sigh and did as he was told. Really it wasn't fair. Here he was, being worked into the ground, while all Orinoco did was eat.

'Is very important to take notes,' said Honourable Cousin Tokyo, bowing towards Bungo. 'Great responsibility.'

'I know,' said Bungo in an offhand kind of way. 'Still *somebody* has to do it and, of course, it's *particularly* important to write *Vol. Ten*. Great Uncle Bulgaria couldn't manage it without me, you know. Please carry on.'

'In big cities,' said Honourable Cousin Tokyo, 'we are working in three ways. One is cracker. Allow me to demonstrate.'

He clapped his silky paws and immediately a tiny Womble appeared, carrying what looked rather like a bundle of fireworks. She put it down gently on a square piece of stone, and then took off one of her wooden sandals and hit them sharply. There was a faint fizzing sound and then a *crack, crack, crack* noise, and a very thin cloud of bluey-green vapour appeared. It grew bigger and bigger and thinner and thinner until it vanished altogether.

'Breathe deeply,' commanded Honourable Cousin Tokyo.

The Wimbledon Wombles did as they were told. The air seemed to smell of grass and flowers. It was a very nice smell indeed.

'Is cracker way of getting rid of factory and petrol smells,' said the elderly Womble. 'Works well in small streets. Now show you next way. Come please.' He got up and went to one side of the room and slid back part of the wall. Bungo, holding his notebook, and Orinoco clutching his two wooden sticks, followed obediently.

The view on this side of the burrow was really very pretty indeed. There were a great many small flower beds and tiny trees, all set in terraces with steps which led from one to the next. At the foot of the last set of steps was a large pool.

'Gosh, isn't it tidy?' said Orinoco, licking off the last grain of rice from his paw. 'It's about the tidiest place I've ever seen in my whole life.'

'*Shh*, I'm taking notes,' said Bungo importantly.

'Next, balloons,' said Honourable Cousin Tokyo and he clapped his paws again. Another tiny Womble appeared instantly. She was clutching a great number of strings, and at the end of each string was a large balloon. In fact, if she hadn't been wearing particularly heavy wooden sandals, she might have gone bobbing off up into the sky.

'Let go,' instructed Honourable Cousin Tokyo.

The tiny Womble did as she was told with some relief, and the coloured balloons drifted upwards. Everybody tilted back on their heels to watch them (and in the case of Orinoco nearly over-balanced) and then quite suddenly the balloons swelled up and burst. A faint bluey-green mist appeared and then grew thinner and thinner until it had vanished.

'Gets rid of pollution at middle-high places,' said Honourable Cousin Tokyo. 'However, still problem of topmost high places. So are now working on that.'

'My word,' said Bungo, scribbling away like mad. 'But what goes higher than balloons?'

'Is very good question, young Bungo. Our

138

special vanishing ballons get to certain height and go *fizz, crack, bang*. Workshop has not yet been able to make balloons which go very far up into sky. So . . .' and Honourable Cousin Tokyo bowed deeply in the direction of a very pretty little log hut which had what looked like three roofs, one above the other, so that it strongly resembled a Womble wearing three hats. 'So our most honoured and venerable Workshop Master, Hirado, is now working on stage three, which he will be most pleased to show you. Please.'

'Thank you,' said Orinoco, feeling that something was called for in the way of politeness.

Honourable Cousin Tokyo bowed, so Orinoco bowed back. Everybody then bowed to every- body else and, for a fleeting second, Orinoco suddenly wished that he hadn't eaten quite so much.

A door in the log hut slid open and a Womble with yellowish-grey fur appeared, carrying what looked like a large, travelling trunk made of paper. It had a great many pretty drawings on the side, which reminded Bungo of the cups and plates that Shansi painted for the Wimbledon burrow.

'Workshop Master Hirado,' announced Honourable Cousin Tokyo, bowing all over again.

Hirado returned the bow in a rather brief way. He was wearing a little black silk hat and apron and he had a rather long, grey moustache.

'Ah,' he said, nodding at Orinoco and Bungo, 'we have great problems. *Sssssss*. Who will lend me a paw, hm?'

With his worried look and his abrupt way of talking he made Orinoco and Bungo think instantly of Tobermory and so, of course, they both volunteered at once, because they knew that no

139

Tobermory sort of Womble would stand for any trouble.

'Me,' said Orinoco.

'Me,' said Bungo.

'*Ssss*, quite right too,' agreed Hirado. 'You will be Orinoco, large stout Womble and you . . .' He surveyed Bungo, who gazed back, feeling happier and hardly at all homesick as he waited for the next few words.

'You,' said Hirado, 'are Bungo. Bungo Straits are to south of Japan. Silly sort of name. Very well, open case and take out contents slowly, please.'

With careful fingers they did as they were told, and found themselves unpacking dozens of beautifully made and very delicate paper kites. Attached to the body of each kite was a small tube.

'Now we try experiment,' said Hirado. '*Sssss*. Problem. Problem. You will take string in right and left paw and when I say, you run. OK? One, two, three and now go.'

Down the little steps from terrace to terrace went Orinoco and Bungo, with the strings starting to tug between their fingers.

'Now let out string,' roared Hirado.

Zip, zip, zip, the strings seemed to unwind all on their own. Up went the kites, trailing a little behind to start with and then jerking upwards and further up and up, until they were sailing into the sky.

'Run, run,' ordered Hirado.

Up and down the steps panted the two young Wimbledon Wombles, with Orinoco wishing more than ever he hadn't had three, let along four, helpings of dinner. And up and up and up floated the kites, and very beautiful they looked, as they

140

drifted towards the clouds. They were in all shapes and sizes. Several of them had long tails, while some of them looked like birds and others like snaky dragons.

'Ssss, now!' said Hirado and, as he spoke, the little tubes attached to the kites fell to pieces and the rather yellow sky began to turn green and then blue, until it was the clean washed blue of a summer's day in the middle of the countryside.

'Topmost high places are now clean?' enquired Honourable Cousin Tokyo.

'Sincerely hope so,' replied Hirado. 'Still a few problems to be ironed out, I shouldn't be surprised. That last dragon kite was a bit slow. Well, Orinoco, well, Bungo, am pleased and honoured that you could assist in experiments. You can now stop running about.'

'Actually,' puffed Orinoco, 'I'm quite enjoying it. Never done any kite-flying before. Flew an umbrella once, but it's not the same. Hang on, Bungo, you silly young Womble, you've got that pink boxtail of yours mixed up with my purple dragon.'

'Can't help it,' replied Bungo breathlessly as he thumped past, his eyes fixed on the blue sky above, 'and anyway your purple bird is getting in the way of my green—er—green . . .' Bungo rolled his eyes in the direction of Hirado, who was now writing busily on a beautifully decorated clip-board, which he had taken out of the pocket of his silk apron.

'Green sea serpent, silly young Womble.'

'Green sea serpent, and, Orinoco, do watch that long tail on your yellow butterfly . . .'

'I AM watching . . . whoops . . . sss, problems, problems . . .'

Honourable Cousin Tokyo folded his paws inside the sleeves of his gown, and leant towards Hirado.

'So,' he said gently. 'Congratulations. Am very pleased that these London cousins of ours were here to witness your success.'

'Um,' Hirado scratched behind his ear with his ballpoint pen and watched Orinoco and Bungo who were now running in all directions, laughing and shouting at each other while the kites circled, jerked and flew across the clean blue sky. 'Um. *Sssss*. Not bad little cousins really.'

Honourable Cousin Tokyo agreed, and he and Hirado bowed deeply to each other.

CHAPTER 12

'AH-ROO-AH-ROO-AH-ROO'

'*Ah-roo-ah-roo-ah-roo-ah-roo . . .*' sang Wellington.
'*Ah-roo-ah-roo,*' rumbled Tomsk.
'*Ah-roo . . .*'
'*Ah-roo-ar-roo . . .*'
Wellington took off his spectacles, which had become quite misted up, and wiped them on his shawl. He glanced round at Tomsk who was sitting behind him in the boat.

'*Ah-roo-ar-roo,*' roared Tomsk and dipped the paddle he was grasping too far into the blue water, and the next moment his furry little body was shooting upwards, and then there was a tremendous splash and he vanished in a great surge of bubbles.

'He can swim,' shouted Wellington. '*Ah-roo . . .*'
The long canoe fairly scudded through the water and when Tomsk finally emerged he was quite a long way away, so he took a deep breath and then

began to do his own special Womble-paddle crawl after it. Everybody paddled as hard as they could but, even so, the long canoe and Tomsk reached the shore in a dead heat.

Uncle Dunedin bustled out to meet them. He was a comfortable-looking Womble with light-grey fur and a very pleasant expression. He was wearing a kilt made of grass, and he had a large necklace of seashells round his neck.

'Good day, good day,' he said. 'That was a very good race. You both won. My goodness, Tomsk, you're a fine swimmer.'

'I like swimming quite a lot,' said Tomsk, shaking himself so violently that drops of water went in every direction.

'And I like it here,' said Wellington, climbing out of the canoe. 'It's a very peaceful sort of place, New Zealand.'

'Agreed,' said Uncle Dunedin. 'Come on back to the burrow. Yes, we don't have too many problems here, I have to admit. Sit down, sit down. Our Human Beings are a tidy lot, but I dare say you may have noticed that.'

Wellington took off his shawl, wiped his paws on it and nodded. Of all the countries he had visited so far, he had to admit that he felt most at home in New Zealand; which was strange really, as it was about as far as he and Tomsk had travelled from Wimbledon. And yet, from the very first moment that he had set paw here, he had felt happy and unworried. Which, as Wellington is a terrible worrier, was quite extraordinary.

Tomsk looked round the long, rather low burrow and sighed contentedly.

'You've got skiing and swimming and walking

144

and golfing and cricket and football and rugger,' he said, 'and not much tidying-up work or pollution, so what do you do?'

'Nothing much—we just enjoy ourselves. We sing, we dance, we make carvings, we keep an eye on the tourists and we go out in our boats.'

'It sounds awfully nice,' said Wellington, who felt that, as he had chosen a New Zealand name for himself, he had to be extra-polite, 'but don't you ever get bored?'

'Well, maybe sometimes a little bit,' agreed Uncle Dunedin, 'which is why I've written a few notes for Great Uncle Bulgaria. I expect you'd like to see them. I've got 'em here, somewhere . . .'

He opened and shut all the drawers in his desk, and in the last drawer of all he found what he was looking for. It was an enormous sheaf of notes.

'It's the whole history of the New Zealand Wombles, North and South Islands, over the last few hundred years. I dare say there's a little too much there at the moment, but you, Wellington, will be able to get 'em into shape, I expect?'

'Lumme,' said Wellington before he could stop himself. 'Sorry, I mean it looks like rather a long job, you know.'

'Mmm,' agreed Tomsk. As it takes him about half an hour to read one page in a book (even his favourite book which is called *Putting and The Advanced Golfer*), he knew quite well that he, at least, would never be able to get through all those notes; so he very wisely kept quiet and left it to Wellington to deal with the situation.

Uncle Dunedin's face fell, he sighed a little and began to gather up the great stack of papers. It was quite obvious that his feelings had been rather

145

hurt, although he was trying not to show it.

'I'm sure it's all very interesting,' said Wellington, 'and I do hope you won't think I'm being rude . . .'

What is he going to say? thought Tomsk, swallowing with embarrassment and shuffling his paws.

'But,' went on Wellington calmly, 'I know that Tomsk and I would find it even nicer and more exciting if you could *tell* the story to us. It's been smashing listening to you telling stories round the fire at night. So could you? Would you?'

'Yes, do!' agreed Tomsk, beaming at this brilliant idea of Wellington's. Remarkable sort of Womble, Wellington. Always came up with the right answer in the nick of time.

'You don't really mean it,' said Uncle Dunedin, looking quite shy himself, 'do you?'

'YES. Please.'

'OK then. Tonight after supper, all right?'

So that evening after a simply sumptuous supper, which included Rotorua moss casserole and Wanaka waterweed cream ices, every single Womble of the North Island Burrow sat round in a circle. They were all wearing their best cloaks and shell necklaces and they swayed from side to side, gently clapping their paws and singing softly.

'Ah—roo-ah-roo-ah-roo-er-roo . . .'

A full moon rose slowly, dimming the lights of the sparkling stars. There was the very faintest breeze off the sea and some night birds were calling to each other.

'I don't wonder this is marked as a three-star

146

burrow,' said Tomsk. 'I think it should be three and a half stars, myself.'

'*Shh*, sorry, but here comes Uncle Dunedin. I say, doesn't he look splendid!'

The singing grew louder and louder and then ended suddenly in a kind of shout, as Uncle Dunedin, wearing his very best outfit, walked into the centre of the ring. He nodded politely to everybody and then sat down on a carved stool. For a moment you could have heard a shell drop, and then he began to talk.

'Once long, long ago there were the two islands, the great mountains, the great lakes and many strange wonderful birds such as the kiwi and the moa. The mysterious thing about these birds was that they had no wings, so of course they couldn't fly. They were very large and they roamed where they pleased, sometimes stopping to pass the time of day with the Wombles.

'Now the Wombles of those long ago days had no tidying-up work to do at all. This was because there were no Human Beings either in the North Island or the South Island. So they spent part of their time caring for animals or birds that were in trouble, and occasionally helping a stranded fish out to sea again. And the rest of the day they swam and climbed and played games and cooked delicious meals. And of course they talked and told stories. It was a very beautiful life.'

'It must have been,' said Wellington with a sigh.

'Then suddenly everything changed. One day the seabirds rose up in great clouds and began to fly round and round. The Wombles hurried to see what was the matter, and at first they didn't understand what was happening at all, for the seabirds were too frightened to explain themselves. But the Old Womble Chief felt his fur begin to rise up, and he knew that something dreadful was about to take place. He looked out to sea and there on the horizon was a sight which even he, wise though he was, didn't understand. It was as if a great tide of hollow tree trunks was moving over the water and towards the land. Sitting inside the hollow trees were funny-looking creatures. They had no fur and they were long and thin, and they had pieces of wood in their front paws.

'The old Womble Chief didn't like the look of these creatures at all, and he ordered all his Wombles to go and warn the moas and the kiwis and the animals to take cover. But the animals and the birds didn't understand because, you see, they had never been frightened in their lives. They had always lived together quite happily and in peace. So, instead of taking the Wombles' warning many of them went down to the seashore. The seabirds, who already knew better, because some of them had travelled great distances and been to other lands where they had seen these fur-less, thin creatures, tried to sound the alarm too. But already it was too late. One of the creatures stood up in his tree trunk and threw a piece of wood at a moa. It pierced the great bird to the heart and it fell dead.

'So the first Human Beings came to this country. They were fierce and cruel and they slaughtered the wingless birds until there were hardly any left. They even killed many of the birds which could fly, and they hunted the animals as well. It was then, for the first time in their history, that our Wombles started to build burrows and to live underground.

'A long time later more Human Beings, also travelling by canoes, came from the sea to the north. They were much more peaceful by nature and they danced and sang a great deal, but by then all the remaining birds and animals were frightened of Human Beings and the Wombles had decided to keep themselves to themselves.

'This was just as well for, as the years passed, there was a third invasion and this time the Human Beings came in big ships, bringing not only their own animals with them, but guns and gunpowder as well. It was these Human Beings who built the towns and harbours, the roads and finally the airports. They were untidy and wasteful, and the Wombles were so upset at seeing what was happening to their beautiful country that they decided to begin tidying- up work, and to make good use of bad rubbish. This is the story of our two islands.'

'It's still a very beautiful country,' said Wellington. 'I think it's the most beautiful one I've seen.'

'Thank you,' said Uncle Dunedin. 'You must tell Great Uncle Bulgaria that we shall do our best to keep it as beautiful as we can. But now, before we go to sleep for the night, my Wombles are going to do a dance for you, which they learnt from watching the Human Beings who came in great canoes from the north . . .'

Uncle Dunedin clapped his paws and all the Wombles, even the very small ones, got up and formed themselves into lines. They began to sway backwards and forwards and to hum softly and in a few minutes, without quite knowing how it happened, Wellington and Tomsk were joining in.

'*Ah-roo-ah-roo-ah-roo-ER-ROO* . . .' rumbled Tomsk.

'*Ah-roo-ah-roo*,' chanted Wellington, 'and oh, I say, Uncle Dunedin, thank you very much for telling us that story. I did enjoy it, even if it was a bit sad. *Ah-roo-ah-roo* . . .'

CHAPTER 12½

WELCOME HOME

'Shouldn't be long now,' said Great Uncle Bulgaria, looking at the alarm clock which he always kept in the back pocket of his shawl. 'I must say I have missed our four brave volunteers.'

'Been a bit quiet without 'em, I admit,' agreed Tobermory, staring in some perplexity at the two pieces of paper which had just come off the Womblex machine. 'The first one says, "Two right young Wombles you've got there. Tomsk will make good pace bowler and Wellington certainly knows his own mind. Stop. Regards from down Down Under. Great-great Aunt Matilda Murrumbidgee. Regards to Young Bulgaria and Botany." What do you make of *that*, Bulgaria?'

'Waltzing Matilda, I believe they used to call her in her younger days. It's perfectly straightforward. Wellington and Tomsk have made a very good impression and have helped to Keep Australia

Beautiful. Quite right too, so they should,' replied Great Uncle Bulgaria, trying not to sound immensely proud of his young Wombles and not succeeding in the least. 'What's the second Womblex message say?'

'Ah-HEM. "Boxes, balloons, crackers, butterflies, birds, dragons send humblest paw greetings to all relations, particularly Honourable Bulgaria and Tobermory. Stout Orinoco—well, they've got him right anyway . . . sorry—and young Bungo. Fine Wombles. Humbly Tokyo." Well?'

'I'm not too sure where the dragons and butterflies come into it, but the rest of the message is plain enough. Orinoco and Bungo have acquitted themselves well. I always knew they would.'

'Can you see them yet, Monsieur Bulgaria?' asked Madame Cholet, bustling out of the burrow and wiping her hands on a cloth. 'My extra-extra-special meal is almost cooked.'

'Not yet, Madame Cholet. But don't worry. We have Womble pickets posted all over the Common and, at the first sighting of a balloon, they will bring news to me at double-quick speed. I will then ring this bell to summon everybody else.'

'Tiens,' said Madame Cholet, 'les pauvres little Wombles. I expect they will be starving, especially that Orinoco . . .'

She hurried back into the burrow, passing Miss Adelaide who was marshalling the smallest members of the Womblegarten into a crocodile. They were whispering and pushing and shoving, their little eyes positively glowing with excitement.

'Form up,' ordered Miss Adelaide. She nodded politely to Great Uncle Bulgaria. 'We are planning a little surprise for the returning travellers. Excuse us. Womblegarten, move forwards and quietly, quietly, please.'

Alderney and Shansi, who were two of the pickets, were for once quite unable to talk as they watched the sun come up slowly, turning the grass on the Common to red, then yellow and then finally restoring it to its natural green. All the trees were in full leaf, the squirrels were busy hopping from branch to branch and the birds were just trying out a few scales before launching into their full dawn chorus. The badger came snuffling and snuffling out of his sett, blinked and looked up at the sky, his paws twitching. Even placid Cousin Botany found himself quite unable to concentrate on potting out, and had abandoned his little greenhouse; he too was staring up into the sky, as he muttered under his breath, 'Well, come on then, young Wombles, where are you then . . . ? *Tsk, tsk, tsk . . .*'

The Womblex machine tapped quietly to itself in the Workshop, and Tobermory went to look at it briefly and came back mumbling.

'Only Yellowstone again. Sends three Womblex messages a day, he does. Gabble, gabble, gabble as I . . . Hallo, what's that?'

Tobermory might be getting on in years, but his hearing was as sharp as ever, and he thought just for a second that he had heard a distant shout.

Great Uncle Bulgaria glanced at his old friend and, seeing how very nervous and on edge he was, said quietly, 'Most interesting that message which suddenly appeared on the Womblex, when it wasn't even switched on. I must admit that I have only distant memories of Dalai Gartok. I

153

remember Quetta Womble telling Yellowstone of the rumours that there were Great White Wombles up in the Himalayas. That was many years ago, of course. I shall be particularly interested to discover what Dalai's silent message meant. Now, how did it go?'

' "Greetings. All pawprints now vanished. Much gratitude. Dalai Gartok and Many Cousins",' said Tobermory briefly. He took off his bowler hat and fanned his face, puffing out his cheeks and shifting from foot to foot. 'Certain I heard something a second ago . . .'

'And how enterprising of Wellington and Tomsk to discover the long-lost Black Forest Burrow and our most distinguished Womble historian ever. I remember . . .'

'*Shhhh*,' said Tobermory fiercely. 'Listen.'

Far across on the other side of the Common Shansi let out a really loud cry for her. Her bright little eyes had just spotted a globe-like shape billowing across the sky.

'Is Orinoco, is Bungo!'

And off across the grass went Shansi, going like the wind, and at almost the same second Alderney picked out a second balloon sailing over the rooftops and she went, 'Yippee, HOORAY! Wellington and Tomsk.'

Away went Alderney with her streamers flying in the breeze and, as though this was a signal for the birds, they stopped practising their scales and began to sing as loudly as they could.

'Here they come,' said Tobermory, waving his bowler. 'Gound the song, Bulgaria. I mean, sound the gong.'

Boooooooooing . . .

Wombles everywhere stopped what they were doing and raced like furry shadows across the Common, so that the two sets of balloonists, who were almost beside their four selves with excitement, saw exactly what was happening. And they jumped up and down, hit each other on the back and, in the case of Tomsk, very nearly stepped back and jammed the automatic landing gear.

'Look, there's Orinoco and Bungo,' exclaimed Wellington, pointing ahead as Balloon One veered across over the top of some trees about a hundred yards away. 'OI, BUNGO, ORINOCO, IT'S US!'

But Orinoco and Bungo were too busy shouting and yelling and dancing about to hear anything but the sound of their own voices. Wellington put Balloon Two on full power, and they slowly gained on their friends, until they were only a dozen yards behind them, as Orinoco and Bungo began to descend. At which point Miss Adelaide, who alone of all the Wimbledon Wombles was perfectly calm, gave a signal and each little member of the Womblegarten scurried about and then stopped absolutely still. Their tubby little bodies made long, but rapidly shortening shadows across the glittering, dew-covered grass, and to the four Wombles up above the shapes of the small Wombles below had formed the words:

WELCOME HOME

'We're home,' said Wellington, rubbing the back of his front paw across his nose. 'I say, Tomsk, old Womble, we're home!'

'Mmm. Nice, isn't it? Mmmm,' said Tomsk.

155

'Oh, isn't Wimbledon beautiful?' said Bungo. 'I like being brave and adventurous and visiting other Wombles, but I'll tell you what, Wimbledon is best!'

'I think,' said Great Uncle Bulgaria to Tobermory, 'that this is one of the proudest moments of my very long life. But my word what a lot of work lies ahead of us. *Vol. Ten*, thanks to Orinoco, Wellington, Tomsk and young Bungo, is going to be the very best volume in the whole of our history. Ho-hum. I'm sorry, you were saying something?'

Tobermory put his bowler hat on again, went '*tsk, tsk, tsk*' and moved forwards to help with the final landing.

'I was saying, Bulgaria,' he said over his shoulder, 'that I'm willing to bet two dozen of Madame Cholet's extra-special daisy cream buns to an empty tidy-bag that I know what Orinoco's first words will be on landing. He may have had adventures all round the world, but it won't have altered *him* one tiny bit!'

Rather stiffly the four young Wombles climbed out of the trolleys, shivering and shaking a little with excitement and relief.

'Whoops!' said Bungo as the Common seemed to roll up and down under his back paws, and he made a grab for Tomsk who, of all four of them, seemed to be steadiest on his feet. 'I'll tell you what, old Womble,' Bungo went on, 'it's jolly nice to see you again, and old Wellington as well.'

'Mmmm. Ditto,' rumbled Tomsk.

'Sorry, yes, I say, rather, oh dear, YES!' agreed Wellington. 'And it's smashing to see everybody else too, isn't it, Orinoco?'

156

Orinoco nodded, sniffed the morning air, stretched and then very slowly a look of pure happiness crossed his round face, and he sniffed again even more deeply as he watched all his Wimbledon Womble relations hurrying towards them.

Great Uncle Bulgaria was in the lead with both his front paws held out in welcome, and close behind him was Tobermory, who was frowning horribly so as not to show how enormously pleased he was. The Womblegarten were all jumping up and down and hitting each other on the back and turning somersaults; and Miss Adelaide, for once, had quite given up trying to control them, as she busily polished her spectacles on the edge of her shawl. Cousin Botany was ambling along at the back of the crowd with a flowerpot in one paw and a trowel in the other; and Madame Cholet was standing in the doorway of the burrow, clasping an enormous mixing bowl which she seemed quite unable to put down.

As for Alderney and Shansi they were clinging together like two furry little limpets.

'I say, Orinoco,' said Bungo, 'there's really no need to be upset, you know. We're back safe and sound. You can stop sniffing.'

'Upset? Who's upset?' said Orinoco, mildly surprised. 'Can't you smell what I can, you silly young Womble? It's Madame Cholet's extra special stew and I'M STARVING!'

'I owe me two dozen extra special daisy cream buns,' said Tobermory to nobody in particular, and he actually smiled from ear to ear.

'*Shhh*, hush, *shhh!*' commanded Great Uncle Bulgaria, raising his white paws. 'I have a Little

Announcement to make on this Momentous Occasion!'

Everybody stopped shouting, cheering and chattering and there was silence, except for the birds and the faint rumbling of Orinoco's stomach.

Great Uncle Bulgaria took a deep breath and made the shortest speech of his long, long life. It was, 'Orinoco, Tomsk, Wellington, Bungo— WELCOME HOME!'